L

COUNTESS IN
COWBOY BOOTS

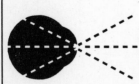

This Large Print Book carries the Seal of Approval of N.A.V.H.

COUNTESS IN COWBOY BOOTS

JODI O'DONNELL

THORNDIKE PRESS
A part of Gale, Cengage Learning

Detroit • New York • San Francisco • New Haven, Conn • Waterville, Maine • London

GALE
CENGAGE Learning®

LIBRARY OF CONGRESS CATALOGING-IN-PUBLICATION DATA

O'Donnell, Jodi.
  [Cowboy boots and glass slippers]
  Countess in cowboy boots / by Jodi O'Donnell. — Large Print edition.
    pages cm. — (Thorndike Press Large Print Clean Reads)
  "Originally published as COWBOY BOOTS AND GLASS SLIPPERS"—T.p.
verso.
  ISBN 978-1-4104-5848-3 (hardcover) — ISBN 1-4104-5848-2 (hardcover)
  1. Large type books. I. Title.
PS3615.D659C68 2013
813'.6—dc23   2013005564

Published in 2013 by arrangement with Harlequin Books S.A.

Printed in the United States of America
1 2 3 4 5 6 7 17 16 15 14 13

For Dad, the last of the good guys

CHAPTER ONE

Lacey McCoy opened the cab to the Dodge Ram pickup and climbed inside, careful to close the door gently behind her, partly out of deference to her father's pride and joy. Mostly, though, it was because the pickup sat directly on Main Street in Abysmal, Texas, population two thousand and change, and any kind of an angry scene would be sure to send jaws slackening and tongues wagging all up and down the way.

Hardly what she needed when she was trying to become regular Lacey McCoy again and blend back into the rural Texas scenery.

Besides, she had learned in the past several months that when this desperate, clutching, trapped feeling came upon her, it was best for her to step out of the stream of life for a few moments and focus on being inside her own skin. It was just a whole lot easier on her than trying to make someone understand why she had just blown up at them, when their not understanding was the reason she'd done so in the first place.

But as life often goes, she was not to be allowed the indulgence of putting her mind in order before being shoved back out on the hairy end of the stick.

For in the next second the passenger door of the truck swung open, sending her heart pounding out of her chest in direct opposition to her efforts to compose herself.

In climbed a tall, grim man. He closed the door behind him, then looked at her with pale-gray eyes as cold as glacier ice.

"Drive," he ordered.

"What the —"

He reached across and turned the key in the ignition. A large boot shoved hers off the brake pedal. He yanked the gear shift into Drive, then switched his foot to the gas. He'd steered them one-handedly out of her parking space and halfway down Main Street before Lacey could scarce gather her wits.

When she did, she took hold of the wheel with both hands and stomped on the brakes, hurtling them both toward the dash as the engine revved and the tires screeched. And people stared. Old Man Wilkins, from his standard post on the bench in front of Smitty's Barbershop, looked about ready to drop his teeth, and Lacey caught the flash of Vernal Adams's bright red beehive poking through the doorway of the drugstore before she disappeared again. The phone lines were probably already burning up.

Lacey could see the headline in the *Abysmal Times* now! "Brake-Stands For Returning Royalty: Ex-Countess Lacey Laslo Lays Rubber On Main." *Exactly* what she needed when she was trying to convince everyone she was "just folks" and making a stab at getting a job here.

On the other hand, maybe she ought to thank this man for making her feel part and parcel of this town. Because acting like he owned Abysmal and everyone in it was vintage Will Proffitt.

"Take your foot off the gas!" Lacey directed, furious.

Will complied, releasing the wheel as well, palms held up, as if all she'd had to do was ask.

She took control of the Dodge with a cutting glare that made not a scratch on the surface of his impenetrable self-assurance. In fact, Will Proffitt settled into his seat with the air of a man making himself at home. Any attempt to eject him from the cab of the pickup would be futile, she knew.

Her best option was to take this somewhere else.

A few minutes later, Lacey pulled up at a deserted street corner and cut the engine. For a moment, she merely sat there, her fingers curled around the steering wheel as she fought to bring her breathing back to normal. It was by no stretch of the imagination an easy task. And she didn't like that one bit.

Finally, she managed a calm "Hello, Will."

" 'Lo, Lacey." He braced the toe of one scarred, dusty cowboy boot on the center console of her father's pride and joy in a way that immediately raked up her resentment. Acting like he *owned* it. But she slanted him as cool an appraisal as he'd given her a few minutes before.

He wore a Western shirt rolled up at the sleeves, faded-to-gray Wranglers worn down at the cuff, and a sweat-stained straw Stetson pulled low on his brow. Just your everyday, ordinary man-about-the-ranch. You'd never have known by looking at him that Will Proffitt owned the biggest cattle operation in the tri-county area.

Except for the way he filled the cab of the truck with his long frame and sharp angles and sheer force of character. He'd always bore a strong presence, especially backed up as it'd been by that combination of money, power, and honest-to-God magnetism. But now Lacey saw how, in her eight-year absence from Texas, he'd become even more riveting, a composition of sinew on bone and features chiseled over time which were a testimony to his survival in the face of the Panhandle's sand-blasting wind and nail-driving rain and brain-baking sun.

He looked cut from stone — and just as invulnerable.

A spark of some emotion seeming much too close to fear sizzled a path up Lacey's spine. She'd have given her right arm for a moment to collect herself, but it wasn't to be hers.

Well, then, she'd have to get through this. And she must remember: she had a pretty formidable layer of bedrock running through her, too.

"You mind telling me what that little performance back there on Main was about?" she asked.

"No performance. I merely wanted to have my own private audience with the countess and didn't think you'd want to do that smack in the middle of town with the whole of Abysmal watching." He lifted his eyebrows. "Was I wrong?"

"Well, you certainly threw any chance for privacy right out the window by drawing all that attention to yourself," she pointed out.

"*I* drew attention to myself? What do you call the way you've been seen at the café with my brother lookin' like cozy itself? Now *there's* a performance."

Lacey barely managed to keep her mouth from falling open at his gall.

Lee Proffitt had been about the only person in town to give her any encouragement in her aim to make a normal life for herself here in Texas. In fact, not a half hour ago at the café he'd told her, with some mysteriousness, that if she could just sit tight for a few days, he could offer her a job at the tack-and-feed store he managed.

Except Lacey found she'd just as soon not have to avail herself of Lee's offer. Something didn't quite feel right about it, which was the best she could pin it down to at the moment.

Then it hit her. Of course. *Here* was the reason for her feeling skittish about Lee's assurances. How could she have forgotten his older brother and the iron rein Will seemed to hold on Lee and the rest of this town? In fact, that had become his nickname, she'd learned since returning, murmured behind his back with some amount of awe and fear: Iron Will Proffitt.

And now he was looking at her as if to

mesmerize her, too, making Lacey feel like a deer caught in the crosshairs of a wolf's gray-eyed sight.

Another quiver of apprehension shot through her, which she tamped down with all her might. She couldn't let this man get the better of her.

"Lee and I have had a few chats, if that's what you mean," she answered guardedly. "He's been a real help to me since I got back."

"And who wouldn't jump to do the bidding of America's Cinderella, right?"

She gritted her teeth at *her* nickname, conferred upon her eight years ago by a media anxious to cater to the public's feeding frenzy for all things royal.

No *way* would she give Will Proffitt the satisfaction of seeing what a crazy-maker the whole situation still was for her.

"I'm sure I have no idea what you're getting at," Lacey said with a lift of her chin. "You know that Lee and I have always been close, and I'm appreciative of him wanting to renew the friendship, especially when I didn't come back to Abysmal once after I left. Although it wasn't because I didn't want to," she finished revealingly, barely having time to wonder why since Will fairly snorted his disbelief in reaction.

"Oh, come on," he said. "You don't expect me to believe you even thought of lookin' back once you shook off the dust of this town. And now you've got the nerve to come back actin' like bygones'll sashay right by, after the way that Lee practically —"

He broke off, which made Lacey ask, "What about Lee?"

But he merely bent that intent scrutiny on her again. "Nothin'," he finally said. "Just answer me one question — are you leadin' my brother on?"

There was simply no getting past it: his accusing tone just irked the life out of her. A better woman would have continued to ignore it, would have risen above it. But Lacey never claimed to be candidate for sainthood even on her best days.

Call her reaction rash or what have you, but some fire starter inside her made Lacey ask, "All right, what if I am?"

At that, Will's face did turn to stone. He bent toward her, one arm sliding along the seat back behind her, the other braced against the dash. "I'll say it once, Lacey — stay away from Lee."

The door handle dug into her back but she refused to be cowed by him. "How could it possibly be any of your business?"

"Oh, it's my business, all right," he

14

drawled. Up close like this, the force of his will virtually radiated from him. "For starters, it was made my business when I got a call from Lee last night sayin' he'd taken a crack at redoing the financial projections on the tack and feed and according to his calculations there was plenty of room for another full-time store clerk, includin' perks!"

Lacey shook her head, trying not to let his proximity overwhelm her. "Lee mentioned something about a job to me, but I didn't ask him for one, if that's what you're thinking, and I don't expect it, either!"

"Now I can believe that. The countess workin' at a tack and feed? How unrefined." His face was still inches away, and she saw his lashes flicker as his gaze took her in. "But then, the offer of a job probably wasn't what you were hopin' for when you called Lee up to fill his ear and tug on all his heartstrings with your troubles, now was it?"

He really had a talent for ticking her off. With effort, Lacey held on to her composure, but with as much narrow thinking along the same lines as she'd had to contend with this morning, she was perilously close to giving this man a considerable piece of her own mind.

"Now wait a minute," she said, not liking

that she sounded defensive, irritated that she was having to be so. "Lee's the one who called *me* when I first got to town a few days ago to offer his help as an old friend."

She was to the point of not bothering to hide the accusation in her own voice as she continued, "Besides, if what you're saying is true, and Lee is makin' promises you'd rather not have him make, why aren't you calling him on the carpet instead of me?"

"I did, last night." Will's mouth thinned as he sat back in disgust, and Lacey drew her first full breath in two minutes. "He pretty much said what you did, that he was just trying to make you feel welcome after going through a divorce, helpin' you out as you get yourself settled. And finding a job."

He gave a short laugh. "I still think that is one fine touch, you needing to find work. It'll be a tough bill to fill, believe me, with or without Lee's help. Not much call in Abysmal these days for countesses."

Lacey clamped down on her jaw. She would *not* respond to his digs.

"For your information," she stated as impassively as she would have read a prepared statement to the media, "I am no longer the Countess Laslo."

"Do tell." He studied her the way he had before, watchful steel-gray eyes keen upon her face, which this time she kept as blank and smooth and impervious as a concrete wall.

It was, she realized suddenly, a mask she'd perfected over eight years, a defense mechanism she'd learned well at Nicolai Laslo's hand: detach, withdraw, hold back any feelings which you might be disapproved of for showing or, worse, might be used against you.

That trapped, desperate feeling clutched at her throat.

How dare Will Proffitt set off such a reaction in her! She couldn't let that part of her life follow her here. She simply couldn't.

"Honest, Will, there's nothing between Lee and me," Lacey said with all the reasonableness she could muster. "We're friends and that's all. I'm not angling for anything with him. All I want is just to be Lacey McCoy again."

He raised an eyebrow. "So are you saying you *haven't* come back to find a man to latch on to so you can keep avoiding taking responsibility for your actions, and Lee's easy pickin's? 'Cause a few minutes ago you as good as admitted you had."

"I was just being contrary!" She gave a huff of pure frustration. "And just where are you getting this idea that I'm avoiding responsibility and looking for someone to bail me out?"

"Oh, I don't know. Maybe it's how hardly a week went by in the past eight years when your mother didn't place some news item in the *Times* relating yet another chapter in the lives of the jet-setting count and countess and carrying on about your parents' trips to this French chateau or that London town house. No detail was spared, believe me, and it was obvious you were havin' the time of your life. So don't expect me to believe you've given up the fairy tale, Cinderella."

She was not going to respond to that name! But instead of stifling her reaction this time, Lacey glowered at Will, and the stare-down they engaged in went on a full minute.

Yet she found her gaze dropping to escape the unrelenting scrutiny of his, realizing that while she didn't want to hide herself behind a mask, neither did she want to give this man even the slightest access to her thoughts.

For there was no telling what he'd make of the truth which no one knew, of how nightmarish the fairy tale had grown, how midnight had finally tolled, turning the golden carriage back into a rotting, empty

18

pumpkin, the fawning coachmen back to vermin, the riches back to rags. The happiness to a disillusionment as bitter as the taste of cinders.

No, she hadn't told anyone, mostly because she had an idea that people would find it difficult to understand what it had been like for her, suspected that they'd be too dazzled by the gilding on the cage to look past it to the crushing loneliness residing within.

And she had even more of an idea that Will Proffitt, master of all he surveyed, would understand least of all.

Lacey met Will's gaze straight on. "You do realize, Will, how completely ridiculous this whole conversation is. Lee and I are grown adults who can think for ourselves."

"Lee's a good man who has a history of lettin' his affections get the better of his judgment."

Boy, he'd argue with a stump! "Fine! Say there is something to your concerns —"

"Oh, there's somethin', Cinderella, believe me."

Her fingers dug into her thigh. "And *if* there is," she continued, "I still don't see why you won't let Lee handle it himself, because really, I'm not out to pull anything over on him. I'll find a job on my own, believe me."

"I'm not takin' that chance. I mean, look at it from my side, like how I'm wonderin' what it was you could've done that Laslo took away your tiara and managed to escape settling a big fat divorce settlement on you so you had no choice but to come back to Abysmal."

That did it. This time Lacey stuck her nose practically up against his. "Believe me, I had a choice, although if I'd known I'd have to deal with an interfering, domineering ring-tailed control freak like you, I would have settled anywhere but here!"

"Yeah?" He looked clearly furious with that assessment of his personality. "Well, I was born in the dark, Cinderella, but it wasn't yesterday."

"And stop calling me Cinderella!"

She didn't realize how vehement she'd sounded until her words were reverberating in the truck's cab. Will studied her impassively.

"But that's what you are and always will be to Lee," he said, "and to everyone else in this town."

His statement stunned her, because she was much afraid he was right. Stunned her, frustrated her — and made her mad.

"Well, obviously if I can convince *you* I'm

20

not," she retorted, "then the two thousand, one hundred and fifty-six other people in Abysmal will follow suit and my work here is done!"

There was another beat of silence and then, to her amazement, Will laughed, a short bark of mirth that clearly said she'd surprised him. It completely changed him, surprising her, too, as the forbidding aspect to his expression fell away, and she caught a rare glimpse of a side of Will Proffitt she'd wager few saw.

For there, in the back of his eyes, she saw a flicker of something — respect? — which somehow eased that constricting band around her throat, ever so slightly.

"Why do you dislike me so much, Will?" Lacey asked candidly. "Of course, you never were exactly friendly when Lee and I were seeing each other, but at least you had a civil word for me whenever we crossed paths. I'd just like to know what it was I did that put such a bad taste in your mouth about me that you'd hold it against me now."

At her question, his gray-eyed gaze shuttered again, and he frowned with such formidable thoroughness she wondered how she'd managed to make him drop that demeanor for even a second. Still, she waited, not knowing why his reply would be so important to her, only that it was.

Yet when he spoke, it was not in answer to her question.

"Lee's happy, Lacey," he said. "For the first time in a long time — I'd say first time since our father died when Lee was just a little kid of eight. He favors Daddy, meanin' they're both of a tender nature, not too good at ridin' the highs and lows life hands out as a matter of course. And sensitive to a fault, givin' the shirt off their backs to anyone who asks for it — and it's been up to me to make sure they didn't lose the ranch in the process."

His eyes turned grim. "And that's the way it'll stay, especially if no *ex*-countess puts notions into Lee's head that he's got a shot at rescuin' her in some outdated code of cowboy honor out of a Louis L'Amour novel."

"For the tenth time, I'm *not* looking for a man to take care of me!" Lacey said.

"That's good, because neither of us Proffitts is in the business any longer of caterin' to any female's needs, unless she's nursin' a calf that's going to bring us a considerable profit come market time!"

Now *he* sounded almost defensive, and that's when the glimmer of a suspicion hit her like the light reflecting off the chrome ram hood ornament. "What's this all about, Will Proffitt? Is there something going on here I don't know about? About Lee?" He'd certainly alluded to some problem with Lee, but then an impulse made her ask, "About *you*?"

She obviously hit some kind of sore spot, for Will turned to stare out the windshield, again not answering her. And for the first time, relieved of that laser gaze, her own was able to examine his face for clues.

Yet she didn't; instead she found her eyes sketching the sweep of his lashes, the slope of his jawline — and the undeniably sensitive curve to his mouth.

She'd never noticed it before, never been close enough to him to have gotten the chance to notice it. And it absolutely captivated her, so novel was the notion that Iron Will Proffitt might have a vulnerable side — just like the one he'd disparaged in his brother.

Fascinated, Lacey found herself focusing on his mouth until another kind of vibration set itself off in her middle. For the first time, she understood how he'd had girls from one end of the Panhandle to the other vying for his attention those years ago.

And now?

Of its own volition, her gaze slid briefly to his left hand, resting on his knee. He wore no wedding ring. So he'd never married? Why? she wondered.

Of course, he *was* Iron Will, a man who made General Patton look like a playground supervisor.

But then there was that mouth. Her attention was drawn back to it, the full bow of his lower lip which dented in at the corners even when his mouth was in repose, neither frowning nor smiling, the last which she'd only seen him do once.

And it had been in response to her.

Lacey glanced up and to her utter mortification found Will's gaze had marked the direction hers had taken. A long moment ticked by in which she saw another kind of flicker flare up in the back of those cool gray eyes, and she realized that somehow, whether she'd wanted to or not, she'd again gotten past that stony, impenetrable exterior of his.

Then his eyebrows lifted in that singular expression of skepticism and he drawled, "Not lookin' for a man, you say? Then why's the needle on my lie detector jumping around like one of those seismographs during an eight-point-nine earthquake?"

On balance, Lacey considered, maybe it

had just been a trick of the light that had made her think this man had even a smidgen of tenderness in his tough hide.

She set her wrist on top of the steering wheel and pointed. "See that road out there? You can take it right out of town and never stop."

His silver eyes merely glinted in amusement as he obligingly opened the door and climbed out as she started the truck, ready to drive him there herself if she had to.

"Y'know, you might be just what this sleepy town needs," he said. "I know I'll be on pins and needles wonderin' what you'll come up with for job skills. Successful yacht lounger? Expert bonbon eater and poodle petter?"

"Well, you can bet I'll come up with something, because if you think I'd *ever* let myself depend on any man again, you don't know Lacey McCoy at all!"

He looked at her through the open window, shaking his head.

"Oh, you may not be America's Cinderella any longer," Will remarked, "but you're sure as shootin' the Queen of Denial."

"Right, and you just let me know when *you* want to get in touch with the real world and I'll patch you through, because the age of overblown Texas cattle barons everybody kowtows to was over about a hundred years ago!"

His eyebrows snapped abruptly together, telling her she'd scored the last point, but it didn't help ease her annoyance as Lacey peeled away in a headline-making squeal of tires and smoking rubber.

A block later she'd slowed down and a few blocks after found another place to park, this time so she could find that moment she so needed to regain her perspective.

She killed the engine and concentrated on regulating her breathing. It helped. Then her gaze dropped to the seat beside her, where lay the local weekly.

Ah yes, the good old *Abysmal Times.* She'd always wondered what brain trust had come up with that masthead, which seemed to suggest the newspaper contained such dire, gloomy reports on life in this West Texas town that only those with extreme intestinal fortitude should risk peeking inside.

But then, the residents of Abysmal had long ago become inured to the connotations of their town's name. If anything, they took the attitude, with true Texan bravado, of someone who's come late to the cattle auction and ends up with the sorriest cow on the yard, only to announce that runty, bowlegged, and big-toe-ugly stock was precisely what he was looking for this season. And he defied anyone to tell him he hadn't gotten a good price, too.

Lacey stared unseeingly at the print before her and realized only then that it was this combination of bred-in-the-bone pride, stubbornness, and God-given certitude which exactly characterized what she had come back hoping to rediscover within herself.

Especially since returning to where and what she'd been was not an option.

So *had* she made the proverbial Freudian slip with Will? Not that she was leading Lee on or that there was anything romantic happening between them, but that what she'd actually come back here looking for was a man to rescue her and take care of her, and had even been doing so all those years ago?

Because it still seemed rather fantastic, even to her, that Nicolai Laslo had come along when he had and had seemed to fit perfectly with her vision of what Prince Charming should be like: handsome, compelling and interesting, but most of all interested in her in a way Lacey had to admit she'd longed for. Certainly, she'd taken the position overseas working as a nanny for the opportunity to see something of the world, but in her heart she *had* been looking for the special once-in-a-lifetime love which she'd somehow doubted would find her back here at home.

And Nicolai had quite simply distracted her with the most convincing facsimile of it that money could buy, romancing her in a way guaranteed to win her heart and confirm what she had secretly wanted to believe all her life: little Lacey McCoy from Abysmal, Texas, deserved high romance with all the trimmings. Deserved that sense of being honored with the best of a man's attention and respect and love. And if that had manifested itself in her being treated like a princess, then was she to blame for responding to Nicolai's flattery and favors and grand gestures?

She still cringed to think of how easily she'd fallen for such blandishments. How she had wanted to be swept off her feet. How she had wanted to be rescued and taken care of.

So did she now? Because she couldn't deny there was something of that nature in the look which had passed between her and Will Proffitt.

Her heart gave an uneven beat as doubt crept up on her and Lacey felt herself reverting to old thought patterns — questioning her judgment, mistrusting the strength of instincts weakened from constantly being twisted and distorted.

That desperateness squeezed at her throat. The feeling was like nothing else in the world; that of being forced to be someone besides herself, but also of not knowing who that person was. And not trusting her judgment as a result.

Lacey felt the tears of sheer terror forming in the back of her throat and made herself take a deep breath. Take a moment to reorient herself. Take a gut check.

And she came up with the answer: Will was wrong. She was *not* back to be rescued by any man. Moreover, she needn't defend herself to that one. She was through with living her life that way. Because of that, she'd *had* no choice, really. Not if she wanted to save her sanity. Save herself. She was meant to do something with her life, and she'd specifically come back here to do it because she knew these people — how they thought, how their minds worked. How their stubbornness continued to wring a living out of this barren land. How they spoke forthrightly, if bluntly, with that God-given certitude which every Texan had learned chapter and verse at the knees of their elders

29

which said their state was better than any other place on the face of the earth.

And how they embodied that bred-in-the-bone pride at being from a little town with the absurd name of Abysmal, Texas.

She'd been one of them once and would be again.

On that thought, she gave the newspaper a snap and set it aside. Yes, she was made of sterner stuff than to throw in the towel — or should she say tiara — just yet. She wouldn't let Will get to her.

Yet in discovering that she could get past that iron guard and glimpse the warmth within, Lacey realized Will Proffitt had done just that.

CHAPTER TWO

Will Proffitt stepped into the cool interior of the Abysmal State Bank, pausing just inside the door to remove his hat and to try to brush at least one layer of West Texas dust off the thighs of his jeans.

Recalling his conversation with Lee last night and the resulting one with Lacey this morning, Will felt his temper hitch up a couple of notches.

He still wasn't quite to believing she really hadn't heard from someone how the news of her engagement eight years ago had nearly destroyed Lee. Or before that how he'd told it around town that as soon as she finished her year-long work visa in Europe, the two of them were the ones going to be married.

Not that Will actually thought his brother and Lacey had had that kind of understanding — Lee was Lee, after all — but she *had* to have had an inkling of how Lee felt about her, enough at least to break her news to him personally!

But no, Lee had learned of Lacey's engagement to Count Nicolai Laslo the way practically the whole world had heard about it, when she'd been dubbed America's Cinderella in that media circus to end all media circuses.

Of course, he hadn't paid much attention to it at the time. He'd been too busy looking for Lee, who'd dealt with the humiliation by disappearing for two weeks.

The muscles along the yoke of Will's shoulder blades tensed at the thought of it. He was of half a mind to relate the incident to Lacey to show her just how much she'd lacked for any kind of human charity, only no way would he hurt his brother that way. Besides, it struck him that if Lacey didn't know about Lee carrying on like a lovesick fool for her, then chances were she wouldn't know of the occasion a number of years after that of Will's own public humiliation when his bride of a year had up and divorced him.

It was just as well the comings and goings of this little jerkwater town on the tail end of Texas held no interest for Lacey McCoy once she'd left it to become the Countess Laslo. Just as well she didn't know how

miserable the Proffitt men were at picking their women and holding on to them.

On that thought, Will headed purposefully toward the back of the building, where beyond the thigh-high wood rail were the offices housing the bank's managers.

"Good morning, Mr. Proffitt," Matt Boyle's assistant chirped in her best school-teacher manner.

" 'Lo there, Missy. Thought I'd drop by for a chat with Matt, if he's not tied up."

"You're in luck, Mr. Proffitt. He's free right now, although I know he'd make time in his schedule for you if he weren't."

"Do tell," Will said mildly. Through the plate glass behind her, he could see Matt sitting with his snakeskin boots propped on a corner of his desk, idly clipping his nails.

Will would have liked not to come to Matt, but he was the senior loan officer for the bank, so Will was obliged to deal with him when it came to handling matters having to do with the tack and feed, which was what he was here for.

"I'll just go on in, if that's all right, Missy," Will murmured, brushing past her to enter Matt's office.

"How do, Matt," he boomed in his best Foghorn Leghorn impression. He stifled a grin as the younger man's boots came off

the desk and hit the floor. The nail clippers made a *ching* as they fell then skittered between two file cabinets.

"Why, Will Proffitt!" Matt said, recovering with a spate of joviality that went with his ex-linebacker-gone-to-seed build. "What a pleasure! Yessir, it sure is!"

Will made no reply. For some reason he was suddenly annoyed. He sat without invitation and got directly to the point.

"You know those transfer of ownership papers I was having you draw up on the tack and feed?" he said.

"They're right here." Matt shuffled through a stack on his desk and came up with a file. He smiled nervously. "Can you believe I was just about to give you a call to see when I could bring them out to the ranch for you and Lee to look at them?"

"Yes, well —" Will scratched the bridge of his nose with the edge of his hat brim "— that's what I wanted to tell you. There's no rush on them. Take your time."

"But they're all in order. Really."

"No doubt there's some details that might benefit from a double check," Will said with heavy emphasis.

"Oh, but it's just a simple transfer of ownership. I've been over the numbers and the wording myself and everything looks

great. All we lack is finishing up," Matt joked. He must have caught the drift of some of Will's growing annoyance, for he added on a stutter, "Th-that is, once the documents meet with *your* approval, of course."

"Of course." Will tried again. "I'm not questionin' your abilities, Matt. I'm just thinking there's no harm in bein' thorough and not rushing the deal, so to speak."

Matt's florid face became even more flushed. "I don't mean to argue with you, Will, but I told Lee just last night when I saw him at the café that the papers were near to being ready to sign. And I'll see him again tonight at darts league. What'm I going to say to him?"

Will sighed. Could the boy really be this obtuse?

"I want you to sit on the matter for a while, Matt," he said. "And I don't want Lee to know. Got that?"

Comprehension was slow to dawn on the younger man but it finally did. "Oh!"

Will reasoned he ought to offer at least some explanation. "Let's just say there's a couple of things Lee and I need to hash out before I'm ready to turn the tack and feed over to him."

"Sure, sure. You can count on my complete discretion," Matt assured him. "Just let me know what else I can do to help, Will."

"I'll do that." Rising, Will gave a nod of dismissal and strode out of Matt's office, more annoyed than ever — with himself, mostly. He could tell he'd just inflated Matt Boyle's sense of self-importance to blimp-size proportions by making him feel like the two of them rubbed shoulders in collusion.

He wasn't doing anything illegal, not even near it!

"Have a good day, Mr. Proffitt," Missy said on his way out.

It struck him then what the situation was he'd registered earlier with Matt: he was given the red carpet treatment wherever he went in this town. Feared and revered — like he was some almighty cattle baron!

Will yanked open the bank's leaded glass door. He'd worked his tail off for nearly twenty years, brought the Double R from the brink of ruin to prosperity, and had done his best to funnel that commerce back through this town. And in his mind, if that brought him the kind of respect which exhibited itself in a bit of fawning in his wake, then he deserved it.

And if he judiciously pulled a few strings to keep one of those he'd worked so hard for from making a foolish mistake, where was the harm?

Of course, Lee wouldn't see it that way.

Will headed up the street to his pickup even as he continued stewing on the matter. Fact was, Lee didn't just favor their daddy, as Will had told Lacey; he was *exactly* like him — prone to following whatever fancy took him, just as Lee had for years on the rodeo circuit.

Which was fine so long as you didn't have a family to support and employees who depended on you, as Art Proffitt had had when he inherited the responsibility for the Double R upon the death of Granddad Clarence.

Will, on the other hand, was more like that man, a hardcore pragmatist with not much patience with such aimlessness. Instead, Will was the type, you saw a job that needed done, you did it.

So it had been when Will, just turned eighteen, had told his father he was taking over managing the ranch. It was either that or lose it. Art just wasn't much of a rancher; it had taken him a mere five years to run it nearly into the ground after decades of Granddad's sound management.

Fortunately, Will had the same knack for ranching as his grandfather. It took a few seasons, but it wasn't long before Will had the Double R breaking even, then soon after that running in the black again, and soon after that expanding. Today, he was a balance sheet millionaire, rich in land and assets.

And when his father had passed on six years ago, he'd done so in the comfort of the home he'd been born in, surrounded by loved ones who truly mourned his passing as one of a dying breed of man, for Art Proffitt had come to be revered as something of a cowboy sage in the area.

While there'd been a time when Will's parents had nearly split up over Art's shortage of direction, Mama had grieved him most of all. So when she'd decided to make another life in Tucson, rather than this tough one on a West Texas ranch, both her sons wished her every happiness.

Will took pride in having had a hand in protecting the happiness of both his parents, just as he found gratification in at last providing Lee with the means to make a steady, reliable living — even if it wasn't, in Lee's mind, the most fulfilling way of doing so.

Will came to a halt in the shade of the awning outside the post office, for there came upon him a squeezing pain in his chest, right in the vicinity of his heart.

There was simply no way he'd let Lee fall for Lacey again.

Because despite her assurance that she wasn't looking for a man, the fact of the matter was Lacey was looking for something. Always had been. And she obviously hadn't found it in Abysmal. Never had — and never would.

Anyone who looked into her wistful green eyes could see it.

Who knew — maybe it had been that look which made a man wonder if he could be the one to make her happy that had captivated Nicolai Laslo, enough to make him want to make her his own. Except Will knew one thing without having it confirmed: no man would ever possess Lacey McCoy. That quiet conviction had radiated from her, much as her pale blond hair haloed her flawless face. And he had almost found himself believing today in the earnestness of her aim to find a job and make a living for herself in Abysmal.

That is, until he'd seen her gaze zero in on his left hand — and then on him. And he almost hadn't felt himself responding, just for one hair-split of a second, to the yearning in those soft green eyes.

What *had* the woman come back here

looking for?

Will took a step, ready to walk away, when through the post office window his attention caught on a square of paper tacked to the bulletin board amongst the Most Wanted posters and Kiwanis meeting notices.

He stepped inside to get a better look and read: Wanted: Job of Any Kind! Must be full-time and pay at least minimum wage. Am a hard worker not afraid to get my hands dirty. Call anytime!

At the bottom it was signed Lacey Mc-Coy.

Will stared at that handwritten note for some time. Any kind of job, was it? And a hard worker not afraid to get her hands dirty. *What about the rest of you?* he wondered with a wry grin.

He reached up and removed the piece of paper, folded it twice and slid it into his shirt pocket before heading for his pickup with renewed gusto.

No point in leaving her ad up there, because he was planning to make Lacey McCoy an offer she couldn't refuse.

The clutching sense of claustrophobia surrounded her like a cloud of noxious gas. In her preoccupation, Lacey had been caught off guard and now found she couldn't draw a full breath.

She had just entered her parents' house.

Very deliberately, she made herself pause and gather her senses in what was becoming a daily ritual since moving home.

Certainly, there was no physical reason to feel closed in. The floor plan was such that one entered the house through a sweeping foyer complete with vaulted ceilings and a cathedral window.

Her back against the front door, Lacey took a tentative sniff. That was it: very faintly came to her nostrils the equilibrium-disturbing sensation of an affluence meant to distract one from the deeper-set atmosphere of declining purpose, dashed hopes and empty dreams.

It smelled, she realized, like her marriage.

Lacey gave herself a mental shake. It was just her imagination. Despite having paid for it lock, stock and barrel, Nicolai had never been in this house; neither had she, for that matter, until a few days ago. Nevertheless, she hustled down the hallway to the friendlier ambience of the French country kitchen, where she found her mother sitting at the table making out a grocery list, a cup of coffee at her elbow.

"Hey, Mom." Lacey glanced hopefully out the window. "Daddy out in his shop?"

"Mmm-hmm," her mother answered, looking ready, in her Western-style skirt and appliqued blouse, for more than a mere dash down to the store.

"Going out?" Lacey asked, automatically opening the fridge to inspect its contents.

"This is my day to get together with the girls for lunch at the café."

"So dinner's catch-as-catch-can for the rest of us, I'm guessing," Lacey remarked.

"Yes. I made up a plate of cold fried chicken for your daddy, but there's plenty left." She cast her daughter a meaningful look. "Just don't expect me to wait on you now."

Lacey straightened. "Have I ever, Mother?"

Rachel didn't answer, but a ridge of flesh appeared between her eyebrows.

Lacey slid a flour tortilla from its plastic bag and munched on it while she rummaged through the refrigerator. Lifting the lid on a saucepan, she found some cooked ranch-style pinto beans. Ah, comfort food. And boy, did she need it, after a morning of futile job hunting, her brush with Will Proffitt, and now her mother in one of these moods.

A bean burrito later, Lacey asked, "Is there anything I can do for you this afternoon? Some laundry or housecleaning? Now's the time to use me, before I've found a job." She smiled at her mother across the table. "It must take some elbow grease to keep this house looking so nice."

"I've been keeping a home for going on thirty-five years, Lacey. I can manage this one fine."

Lacey counted out ten beats as she methodically loaded up another tortilla.

"I wasn't implying you couldn't manage this house, Mother," she said reasonably. "I simply was hoping to make up a little bit for dropping back onto yours and Daddy's doorstep."

"Really, Lacey, I will not see you lowered to cleanin' toilets, here or anywhere else."

This time Lacey required a twenty count as she pondered the logic. So her mother wasn't about to wait on her, yet housework wasn't fit occupation for her.

Rachel continued, "You might make light of the situation, Lacey, but I have to hold my head up in this town. And you comin' back and scrounging for work does not make that easy!"

With a huff, Rachel stood, grabbed up her cup and saucer and went to the sink, where there arose a clatter of utensils and china against porcelain.

Aha, thought Lacey, sitting back in her chair and regarding her mother's stiff spine, *now we're getting down to the heart of the matter.*

For a period of nearly eight years, Rachel McCoy had graced the summit of Olympus, Abysmal-wise. Her daughter, the very fruit of her loins, had married a count — and made national news doing so! Lacey had been hailed America's Cinderella, and Nicolai Laslo her Prince Charming.

Lacey stood also, only she chose to take herself to the window, where she looked out upon a fully landscaped backyard, complete with diving pool.

And then there had been this house. From the first, she had been against the whole idea of building it for her parents. But Nicolai had insisted — and by that time he'd learned where her mother's buttons were and when to push them so that he had her responding to his every hint and suggestion like one of Pavlov's dogs.

Lacey turned, arms crossed over her middle, and regarded her mother. There'd be no good time to bring this subject up, so she might as well get it out and over with. "Mother. I think you better start considering how you and Daddy *are* going to manage this house now that Nicolai won't be paying for its upkeep."

Her mother whirled, her face slack. "He won't?"

She rushed on before Rachel could get up any more of a reaction. "Paying for the expenses on this place — utilities and insurance and taxes and maintenance — is going to take just about all I'm thinking I can earn if not most of what Daddy does, and I'd hate to see you two cutting into your savings to keep this place up."

Her mother shook her head. "We've got the money from the sale of our home two years ago. It's well invested. There's the interest on that we could use. Or we could take an equity loan on this house. That ought to bring us more than enough money."

"But, Mother, you've got to see neither is a practical solution, long-term. You've handled the household budget and the one for Daddy's business for years, so you know it's not sound financially at your age to live off of your interest income. You'd just be robbing Peter to pay Paul by taking out a mortgage on this house."

An idea occurred to Lacey, one that would ease the pressure on her, too, to find a job and allow her to figure out what she wanted to do with the rest of her life. "You know, it'd make a lot of sense to buy a smaller house that's maintainable on what Daddy makes and sell this house and invest the proceeds from it."

"But, Lacey, really —"

"I understand it might feel like a step down in prestige, but honestly, Mother, at a certain point you're going to have to realize that living in a mansion isn't practical for you."

Rachel looked at her strangely. "But, Lacey — just who in Abysmal were you thinkin' this house *would* be practical for?"

Lacey stared at her. Her mother was right. This house was the white elephant of white elephants. There was no one within a hundred-mile radius who could afford it, and even if they could, who'd buy a half-million-dollar mansion in Abysmal, Texas?

How long? How long would she experience these lapses in her reasoning which always seemed to hit her broadside?

Because Nicolai would certainly have foreseen her being put into this position and having to deal with it; she had no doubt he'd planned on it. It was the same kind of calculation he'd used throughout their marriage to keep her within the sphere of his influence — and it seemed he meant to try to hold her there, even though she was no longer married to him.

That desperation clutched at her again, like a vise gripped around her throat. She wouldn't let it get the better of her!

"I have no idea who'd be able to afford this house," Lacey admitted, rubbing her forehead. "So I guess we need to take a look at how to keep it up without you and Daddy going broke. And I won't let you down there, Mother. It's because of me you've got this house, and it's because of my divorce you're stuck with paying for its upkeep, which you never expected to have to do when Nicolai bought it for you."

"Well, I think it's downright dishonorable of him to refuse to!" Rachel said. "I don't know that we'd have accepted the house if we'd an idea we would be saddled with maintaining it."

Lacey knew she'd better get this part out right now. "He didn't refuse. I refused to let him."

Rachel gaped. "Why?"

Dropping her chin to her chest as she thrust her fingers into the front pockets of her jeans, Lacey murmured, "Let's just say I'd rather not have any of us beholden to Nicolai Laslo in any way. It's just . . . how it has to be for me, Mother."

In the ensuing silence, the sound of the

47

central air-conditioning clicking on seemed as loud as a jet engine.

"What did he do to you, Lacey?" her mother asked suddenly.

For a moment, Lacey's eyes stung with tears. She lifted her head, was a step away from going to her mother and finding the comfort and understanding she so needed.

Then she saw it: Rachel stared at her with stark eyes, and she realized her mother wasn't as concerned for her having gone through some ordeal as she was trying to find some explanation for the drastic action Lacey had taken in leaving her marriage.

It almost seemed her mother would rather have had her endure such circumstances than deal with the fact that Lacey had made a choice. And yet she *had* been driven to make one.

Without another word, Lacey strode from the room. She had to — or she'd say something she really, truly would regret.

She came to a halt in the foyer, the sound of her boot heels echoing in the lofty space. Lacey was sure she could hear her thoughts echo as sharply.

It struck her then what else she'd seen in her mother's expression: weariness at her life's work being shown a failure.

The hollowness in Lacey's middle grew to

fill her entire chest. Then and there she vowed she would not let this tragedy carve the same heartache into the planes of her face. She wouldn't cling to old dreams and circumstances, bemoan a past that couldn't be changed, or become brittle with bitterness because the people she'd given control of her happiness had not fulfilled her expectations.

Neither would she withdraw from the world, protect her feelings behind an expressionless mask, within a hardened shell. She'd tried it with Nicolai, and she knew more than ever that she couldn't live that way. What she wanted instead, more than anything in the world, was to live her life as herself, to be accepted for herself. To be loved for herself.

And to love freely, as herself.

There *had* to be some way for her to achieve those goals. However, her first responsibility had to be for her parents' circumstances — which they would not be in right now if not for her.

Lacey clutched the top of the baluster, ready to take the steps two at a time to the top of the stairs and get to the stupid dusting. But she wasn't keen on facing more of the same emptiness. More of the same confinement.

Right now she needed to get away from this place and its stale, stifling air.

Lacey spun, crossed the tile floor in two strides, yanked open the heavy front door —

And plunged straight into Will Proffitt's arms.

Her forehead met his chin with a *crack,* making his hat fly backward off his head. His foot came down on her instep, and she gasped in pain. He gave an "oomph" of his own pain when her elbow connected with his ribs as they both grasped the other for balance.

Her hands spread on his chest, his clasped her waist. Their eyes met in mutual apology.

But neither let go.

Lacey wondered if her gaze was as unguarded as his. For she was immediately caught up in the force that was Will Proffitt.

It was in the feel of him, all solid muscle beneath rough denim and soft chambray. In his untamed auburn hair, thick and wavy and made for twining one's fingers through. Without his hat, his face was completed, the cutting angles of his jaw and nose and cheekbones tempered by the wide brow and those expressive eyebrows. The smell of him was unpretentiously straightforward, an immediate intoxicant combining sweat and outdoors and something pleasantly musky.

Lacey took in one deep lungful of him and felt the last vestiges of the polluted atmosphere disappear from her head. Unable to stop herself, she took another breath. The hollow place in her chest filled to bursting, making her sway.

Will's hands tightened on her waist.

His mouth was directly at eye level, and Lacey found her gaze fixing upon that curve of lip as a slow burn kindled awake in her abdomen, turning into something she hadn't felt in an age: a certain restlessness to reach up and push her fingers through the tangle of dusky hair at his temples as she pressed her mouth against his, just to see, just to feel, just to know if it was as tender as it looked —

Yet on the heels of that sensation came another, reflex-quick, of pure, unadulterated fear. It doused the warmth in one rushing flood.

With a shake of her head, Lacey stepped away from him. Will let her go. His eyes were smoky beneath dense lashes, and she wondered, really, what had been revealed in the depths of hers.

Ducking her chin, she rubbed her forehead. He stooped to pick up his hat and set it on his head before extracting a folded

51

piece of paper from his breast pocket.

Without a word, Will thrust it into her hands.

Puzzled, she opened it and read her ad.

"You serious?" he asked curtly.

Lacey lifted her chin. "As a stroke."

"Well, I can always use hired help at the Double R."

He surprised her. Will Proffitt would have been the last person she'd expect to come to her with an offer of a job.

"Doing what?" she asked suspiciously.

"What d'you think? Working cattle. Moving 'em, dosing 'em, branding 'em — along with the various and sundry other tasks that go with the territory."

His mouth grew determined around the corners. "I'll be frank, it's hard, dirty work, but I'll pay you minimum wage, and if you last the week, you get a dollar an hour raise. Last a month, and you've got another buck an hour. Oh, and you work six days a week, sunup to sundown, time and a half overtime."

She gazed up at him with incredulity. It was an extremely generous offer, especially to someone completely inexperienced at this sort of work.

A feather of gratitude touched her shoulder, making her almost smile at him before

reality clapped its heavy hand on her, bringing her back to her senses.

Will wasn't making this offer to help her.
It was a way for him to earn the right to a
big old I-told-you-so when she balked and
ran away home. A way to make her admit
she couldn't carry her own weight and had
never had the slightest intention of doing
so.

Yet little did he know he was offering her
her freedom. Freedom to be herself for
once, without someone trying to shove her
into the role of a countess.

Of course, Mother would have a veritable
litter of kittens.

"So you want the job or not?" Will asked
impatiently.

She knew nothing about ranching. She'd
be at Will Proffitt's utter mercy. The thought
didn't set well with her at all.

And yet she knew how to handle such
men, which was to give them not an inch.
She *would* handle him.

"You've got a deal," Lacey announced,
and waited for the glint of satisfaction in
Will's eyes at having hooked her.

He merely nodded, looking anything but
pleased.

Then he said, "You do realize the reason
I'm hiring you is so you won't have much

opportunity to, you know, socialize."

"Oh, you mean so I won't get the chance to put a ring in Lee's nose and ride him around like a pet donkey?" Lacey asked with wide eyes. "Actually, that suits me fine. I said it once, I don't need a man to come to my rescue." Using his mode of expression, she cocked an eyebrow. "Rest assured, if one's going to make an idiot of himself, he won't get any help from me."

Ah, there it came, that silver gleam of amusement. And, she would almost have bet on it, of respect.

"Then I'll expect you tomorrow at 6:00 a.m.," he said.

"I'll be there. And I look forward to earning my wages at the Double R."

"You'll sure find out what you're made of," Will drawled.

"Oh? I got the impression that's what you wanted to learn."

And as she brushed past him standing there on the sidewalk, his expression confounded, Lacey couldn't resist tossing a final barb over her shoulder. "Or maybe it's the perfect opportunity for me to find that out about *you.*"

CHAPTER THREE

Hang him if Will didn't take her at her word. Five days into her job on the Double R, Lacey was wondering if she'd have been better off taking her chances at scaring up work in town. She'd never been smellier or dirtier, and she ached in more places than she had places to ache. Even now her left thumb was throbbing with its own heartbeat after getting smashed in a corral gate.

Dropping her hat beside her, Lacey eased herself down against the shady side of the hay barn and leaned back against the rough surface, drinking deeply from the jug of iced tea Will provided for breaks and trying to rid herself of the shakes that had brought her down off the extension ladder.

She'd spent most of the morning in a pen pitching hay into feeders, all the while mired to her ankles in cow pen crud, after which she'd been directed to scrub out and sterilize the birthing stalls. The smell had been stomach-turning and kept her from drawing a full breath for two hours. She'd almost believed she'd been given a reprieve when she was put to work whitewashing the east side of the hay barn, until the sun proceeded to grill her like brisket on the barbecue.

Lacey made a swipe at a pesky fly buzzing around her face before dropping her head forward to better massage the crick in the back of her neck. She didn't know much about ranching, but it didn't take growing up on the Ponderosa for her to figure out she was being given the hardest, lowest and most disgusting of chores. She didn't know how much longer she could maintain this pace, and she was trying hard not to be disappointed in Will because of that. She'd obviously been mistaken about him having even a little sensitivity under that rawhide exterior of his.

On the bright side, such as it was, Will hadn't been around much to see her struggling just to keep up, which was nothing short of a miracle because, she'd learned, Will Proffitt was a hands-on rancher who involved himself in the day-to-day operation of his business.

Which made perfect sense when you inserted "micromanaging control freak" for "hands-on," Lacey thought dourly.

Instead, Will had her reporting to his foreman, Yancy Follett, a Geritol marvel of an old cowboy whose gimlet gaze missed nothing, and he focused it on her with a sharp vigilance, as if she couldn't be trusted not to cheat Will blind. It was an even greater indignity.

But she told herself she could handle it. She couldn't give up yet, at the very least. If nothing else the job got her out of the house and away from her mother's deafening silences.

There'd been the inevitable scene with her mother after Lacey had told both her parents of her new job. Her father had listened to his wife carry on, then had quietly told her their daughter was old enough to know her mind, after which he'd insisted she drive the Ram back and forth to work at the Double R instead of his older truck, which he used for his carpentry business. It was his way of showing his support, and Lacey had understood how much of it he was demonstrating when he'd handed her the keys to the Dodge — his prized possession, one he'd bought and paid for and maintained himself . . . unlike his house.

Lacey hadn't realized until then just what it must have done to her father's pride to have his life's work virtually discounted with the building of that mansion.

But she hadn't seen this until she'd come back.

Lacey rested her forehead upon one bent knee. She didn't know if she'd ever be able to forgive herself for letting Nicolai thrust that house and its contents on her parents. Even knowing how manipulative he was, she hadn't seen how he'd been determined to complete the job he'd started when they married of removing everything familiar and meaningful to her, so she'd have no sense of groundedness or her background or her history. Or her worth, which made her vulnerable to his influence and forced her to depend upon him emotionally, financially and psychologically.

How could she have let him do that to her? She still didn't know. Even allowing herself the naivete of a nineteen-year-old rural girl who'd been raised around Texan forthrightness and had never dealt with any kind of devious purpose in her life, Lacey still faulted herself for not seeing what was really going on.

"There you are," came a deep voice out of the blue, making her jump and drop the jug. It landed on its side, its contents glugging out of it and seeping into the red dirt.

Lacey jerked her head up to find Will

practically standing over her. From this angle, he looked even more imposing than he had in the cab of her father's truck. She'd wager he was six foot six in boots and hat, all of it long, lean legs and wide, sturdy shoulders. And just as she'd concluded, there didn't seem to be a soft spot on or in the man. The expression in his gray eyes was as watchful as ever, as if she were the one trying to pull something over on him. It brought that choking feeling back to her throat.

She'd spent a lot of time in the past few days measuring her distance from Will Proffitt and reassuring herself of the fact that he didn't have anything over any other man on earth, and here he went blowing that theory up in smoke.

"Quit sneaking up on me!" Lacey said crossly, pushing herself to her feet so as to be on a level with him. Every muscle in her body complained but she ignored them and drew herself up to her full height. He still stood a foot taller than her, and at least by this measure she would always have the disadvantage.

Will merely raised one of those thick eyebrows at her accusation. "I'm not over-much given to sneaking up on people. Although if I do surprise someone, it's usually because they were up to something they know they shouldn't be. Any truth in that speculation right now?"

"I'm not slacking off, if that's what you're implying." Lacey took an irritated swing at another fly. "I didn't get a break earlier this morning because you had Yancy putting me through my paces like a draft horse pulling a half-ton payload."

"Not complaining, are you?"

"Oh, I wouldn't dare. I believe in feudal societies complaints are handled rather summarily by disengaging one's head from her body."

The only evidence of her having gotten to him was in the flaring of his nostrils. Then his gray eyes glinted. "That's some kind of vocabulary you picked up when you were married to the count, isn't it, Cinderella? Goes perfect with that high-and-mighty accent and attitude."

Lacey stared at him, barely registering that he'd used that detested nickname. Because he was right; she hadn't noticed before but she was still using the pronunciation and inflection Nicolai had forced upon her during their marriage. She'd despised him for it, despised herself for giving in, even while telling herself she wasn't, not in the way that really mattered, because it didn't change her inside.

But apparently it had or she wouldn't continue to talk this way.

She must have been staring at him pretty dementedly because Will said curtly, "In case you were actually interested in why I stopped, it's because I was passin' by on my way out to one of the south sections and didn't see you up on the ladder, and I was concerned the heat had gotten to you or you'd fallen. If I expected to find anything amiss, it was you passed out cold as a wedge, and now I'm thinkin' there might be something to that concern. You're peaked as a peeled potato and look as clammy."

Though he didn't move abruptly, when he stepped forward as if to lay the back of his fingers on her forehead, Lacey recoiled from his touch as she would a red-hot brand.

She barely took time to note the surprise in his eyes before countering, "Well, you're wrong! I'm just dandy, and I'll get right back to work to prove it." She flipped her work gloves out of the back pocket of her jeans and yanked them on without a clue as to how she'd become quite so angry and defensive and now just plain panicky inside. "But you can take ten minutes out of my paycheck if you still feel I was loafing on your nickel."

"Lacey —" Will said, clear warning in his voice.

"As if there's room for negotiation with you. You've never made any bones about people doing it your way or hitting the highway. Although you probably own that, too!"

She stooped to snatch up her hat and nearly pitched forward at his feet as a wave of vertigo swamped her. Maybe this job *was* too much for her to handle.

Or maybe Will Proffitt was.

Will caught her under the arm with one hand, and the contact brought on another swell of panic which had Lacey jerking away as if she'd indeed been burned.

Straightening, she met Will's eyes and saw the storm gathering in their gray depths.

"Give me a break, Lacey! I'm not going to dock your pay, and I'm not a tyrant over my employees or anyone else, for that matter!"

"Oh, yeah? Then why do they call you Iron Will Proffitt?"

His eyebrows crashed together as lightning struck in those eyes. He stuck out his hand again, to do what this time she had no idea, but there was no controlling her reaction as Lacey jumped back. The move had her losing her balance again. This time Will caught her by both her upper arms to steady her, and the action sent her into full panic mode.

"Let me go!" she cried, pushing at his chest and as close to hysteria as she'd ever been in her life. "You can't control me! You can't! No matter what kind of force you use!"

To his credit, Will immediately dropped his hands. He looked at her with bewilderment and something akin to hurt in his eyes. "Lacey. What kind of man do you take me for?"

"I don't know," she said, shaking her head. "I don't know."

To her horror, tears started in her eyes and she had to press her lips together to stifle a sob.

She must not have been completely successful at it, for Will extended his hand toward her again, then seemed to think better of the gesture. Instead, he took off his hat and yanked his fingers through his sweat-dampened hair.

"I have no idea what's goin' on here, Lacey," he said, with just enough hard-pressed patience that it set her off again.

"That's right, you don't!" she cried. "Men like you run your worlds completely, so why should it come as a surprise that you can barely comprehend what it's like for a woman to fight day after day for what little control over her life she can get!"

His mouth actually fell open. He obviously wasn't expecting *that* from her. She herself hadn't seen it coming until it was out of her mouth. And now that it was, she wasn't sorry to have said it, especially since her outburst made Will look pretty uncomfortable for a few minutes.

Good. It felt very good to get a bit of her own back after years and years of no quarter being given in this debate, not even a nod of acknowledgement for her feelings.

Her fists were clenched at her sides, her arms rigid, and her heart was pounding out of her chest. Oh, she'd needed to say these words, all right, needed to rail on about this circumstance, much of it her own making, she had to admit, for she had handed over control of her life to Nicolai.

So now she was fighting to get it back, and she had to believe she would or she couldn't go on. She *wouldn't* let Nicolai get the better of her! But what Lacey discovered now was that she wasn't yet ready to deal with the real damage she feared he had wrought upon her heart and which seemed to bring on that terrible tightness around her throat.

She half turned away from Will, her arms

crossed and, she was sure, with the most mulish expression on her face as she waited for him to get his bearings back and come up with some pithy zinger which would effectively put her in her place.

Except . . . instead of leveling his steely gaze on her, she saw that Will was actually considering her words. He stood with one hip shot, idly slapping his hat against his thigh.

Then he asked, "So what's it like to feel so . . . vulnerable?"

He surprised her again. Nicolai would have scorned both her emotions and her expressing them, and she'd expected no less from Will.

"At times, it can be terrifying," she found herself answering with brutal truthfulness. "Absolutely terrifying."

"I'll bet it can be," he said simply.

She could detect not one hint of sarcasm in his voice. Nor in his expression. Without his hat on, there was no shading of his features to set them into relief, which made it like looking up at the forbidding face of a mountain at twilight.

Instead, she was momentarily drawn in by the way a damp shock of his auburn hair curved around his forehead, by those thick, straight eyebrows above ridiculously long-lashed eyes. And that crescent lower lip which didn't bear dwelling on.

As before, when she got to him, he got to her.

Lacey spun away, unable to look at him another moment.

The heat was perishing on this side of the barn and out of the wind. Of course, it wasn't as if it brought any cooling effect with it. Both would suck the moisture — and the life — right out of you. Unless you were Will Proffitt; then it made you stronger.

This was his world. What was she doing here? How had she done it again, put herself into an impossible situation of having to meet a man on his own turf? She truly must be demented!

"You're right, Will," she said.

"Beg pardon?"

She turned. "I can't handle this pace and this kind of work. I'm obviously exhausted and a hazard to myself, and it'd be foolish if not dangerous for me to stay in an impossible situation to try and prove I can take it." She'd already spent too much of her life doing that.

"But Yancy says you've worked like a dog. He's got no complaints."

"That's right, because I *have* worked like a dog. But I can't keep it up forever." She dropped her chin so he wouldn't see it trembling. She couldn't keep a lot of things up forever, it seemed.

"If it's because of just now," he said, the timbre of his voice low, "I wasn't going to hurt you, Lacey, I swear."

"Well, after the way you tried to overpower me that first day in my daddy's truck, can you blame me for not knowing that right off the bat?" she asked, looking askance at him.

Now he was the one seeming to take stock of himself, peering at her as if he were just now seeing her for the first time. Finally he said, "You're right. My parents didn't bring me up to browbeat anybody for any reason."

He checked his watch. "It's close enough to noon break that you could stop for dinner. Maybe gettin' a little food into you will be just the thing to revive you."

She frowned in confusion. "But, Will —"

"There's a lot of work to be done this afternoon. I don't need any of my hired hands feelin' poorly."

He stuck his hat back on his head and pivoted away as Lacey stared after him. Hadn't he heard what she said?

"Will —" she started to protest again, but he'd already swung back around.

"Y'know, I've got some orphan calves needin' to be bottle fed and I always have a hard time getting any of the high schoolers we hire for the summer to do it. They'd rather be out in the corral practicing their ropin' skills, and I need someone with patience and a gentle hand for this job."

Scratching one cheek, he squinted at the paltry section she'd managed to get painted. "The barn can wait."

Lacey set her gloved fists on her hips. "But, Will, didn't you hear me?"

"I heard you fine. And I'm willin' to give you another chance —" he cut her a measuring glance "— that is, if you'll give me another chance."

At his words, the chain around her throat slackened a little, and just in time, too. It had gotten so tight in the past few days she wasn't sure she could stand it much longer.

But it was still there, a not-so-gentle reminder that she needed to keep her guard up.

"Look, if this is about keeping me from going to Lee for a job, then you have my word I won't," Lacey said. "Believe me, I don't need that kind of grief in my life."

"Well now, it's not that." He lifted one inimitable eyebrow at her. "I figure I better get you somewheres so I can keep an eye on you, because I frankly don't trust you not to paint Captive Of Iron Will — Send

68

Help! in big white letters on the side of this barn for the whole world to see."

Before she could react, he was off again, impossibly long strides taking him halfway to his pickup in a matter of seconds.

So it seemed Iron Will Proffitt wasn't made of stone. But whether that was good news or bad, she still didn't know.

"Looked like you were havin' a real nice nap from my place up in the choir loft. Had the devil of a time convincin' Ida Thornton not to take it personally, but seeing as how you snored through her entire solo, she wasn't even half for believin' me."

Lacey turned and, walking backward with her Bible clasped schoolgirl-like in front of her, grinned sheepishly at her father as he caught up with her on her way down the street after church.

"I didn't snore!" she averred, knowing better than to hedge on the nodding off part. She *had* been dozing.

"Well, you were sawin' on somethin' pretty hard there," Hank McCoy said, long strides bringing him even with his daughter, whom he embraced in a one-armed hug as she turned back around. They fell into step together. "Like to've drowned out Pastor Mike's sermon on the evils of sloth."

Lacey aimed an elbow at her father's ribs, which he caught handily, giving her arm a squeeze.

A measure of peace settled over her which she hadn't gotten from the service today. But then, she'd always found such comfort in her father's embrace. She loved her mother dearly, but they had never had the special closeness she had with her father.

After years with Nicolai, she badly needed reminding that there were men like her father in this world — good, true-blue men. It wasn't in men like her father to misuse their strength but to hold it in trust for times when it was needed by himself or his loved ones. As with her mother. Lacey had never seen him be anything but respectful and patient with her, even when Rachel hadn't been her best with him.

Lacey studied the cracks in the sidewalk as she stepped over. "Where is Mother, by the way?" she asked.

"Oh, I left her debatin' with the ladies from her civic group," her father answered. "There's the town social comin' up they're sponsoring. Half are wanting music but no dancing, and the other half are sayin' if you have music, people are just goin' to dance. Of course, if you don't have music, then where's the purpose in people going a'tall?"

"Sounds complicated," Lacey said.

"It's a pressing issue, all right. Let's don't even get started on what the status is on whether to serve liquor or not. It ranks right up there with settlin' the nuclear problem."

They both broke out in laughter threaded with well-earned — and fond — tolerance. "You'd think by now Mother would have more of a perspective, wouldn't you?" she said.

"We-ell, left to her own devices, your mother comes out all right in the end. It's just when she's got the press of others' expectations on her that she gets a little off track." Hank shot her a sidelong glance. "Like you with that job."

She should have known her father would bring up the subject.

"Working as a hand on the Double R *is* hard, Daddy," she said a bit defiantly, "but what job can I get here in town? No one's willing to hire America's Cinderella."

"Now, I'm not talkin' about what you're doin' so much as why, although I am after asking Will Proffitt how he thinks workin' you to exhaustion is gonna make up for anything that happened to either his brother or him."

Lacey ground to a halt. "What do you mean? What happened?"

Hank gave his daughter a long look before saying, "No, I'm not one for telling tales that oughta be told by the main players. But I can and will talk about your takin' on responsibility that's not necessarily yours regardin' that house, which is for me and your mother to see to." He took her chin between thumb and forefinger and gave it a shake. "Nobody made us move in there, so I don't want you to take it as your burden."

Her lower lip trembled, and Lacey leaned her cheek against his shoulder to keep her father from seeing it. "But then the question would be, what *will* I do? I want to do something with my life that I not just like to do and am good at, but also believe in."

She worried her bottom lip between her teeth. "I think I *need* to do that. If I could just figure out what that'd be. Right now, though, I need to stick around here and keep working at the Double R so I can help you and Mother," Lacey said.

"I told you, Lacey, you can't worry about that."

"Well, I do! And I'll keep worrying about it until I come up with a way to get the situation under control!"

She slid out from under her father's arm and paced ahead a few steps, trying to get a handle on her emotions. But this was probably the second sorest subject with her right now, and heaven love her father, she just didn't think he'd understand.

Of course, she hadn't thought Will would, either.

Especially yesterday. Yesterday he'd looked straight at her with those intense gray eyes and made her believe. And heaven love *her,* she'd barely stopped herself from letting him past her guard.

The thought that she might both terrified her and set off a romantic in her, almost as much as his touch had done.

She couldn't be so unwise again. Could she?

"Oh, Daddy, I thought coming back here I'd be able to let go and relax about things but it all still seems so hard," she whispered, meaning a whole slew of circumstances, but her father took her as meaning one in particular.

"You don't have to work for Will Proffitt, darlin'."

"Actually . . . actually I think, at least for the time being, that I do," she murmured.

Her father came up behind her, turned her around, and tipped her chin up so she had to look him in the eye. "Things'll work out all right in the end. You'll manage, Lacey. We all will."

"I guess you're right," she said on a sigh. "It'd be nice if we had some kind of idea soon of how we might make that happen."

Hank's hazel eyes twinkled. "I for one am for turning that Panhandle Palace into a boardinghouse."

She had to smile. "Wouldn't Mother love that! You sure you'd want to live with her?"

"Well, now, I've been married to your mother comin' up on thirty years. I figure by now I know how to ride out every kind of storm she can whip up."

He enfolded her in a hug, and Lacey hugged him back. Yes, somehow things would work out, if she could only learn to let go and trust.

But Lacey knew that was easier said than done, especially where Will Proffitt was concerned.

CHAPTER FOUR

It occurred to Will somewhere around the middle of the second week of Lacey's employment that he might have made a serious tactical error.

Leaning his elbows on the top of a gate, he watched her help Yancy load panels of fencing to be used for constructing a temporary chute into the cattle truck. Sweat ringed her armpits halfway down her sides. Her chin-length hair hung lank around a face upon which had there been a speck of makeup, it would have melted off by now. Earlier this morning she'd obviously sat — or fallen down — in something that darkened the entire seat of her jeans.

He'd heard the saying that familiarity bred contempt, but this might be the exception that proved the rule.

She'd decided to continue working at the Double R, and Will took a portion of redemption from that, although he still felt a wave of good old-fashioned shame when he thought about how he'd treated her at first. He still couldn't have said quite why he'd done so, even aside from the situation with Lee.

She'd been as good as her word, too. Lee had told him two days ago she'd told him there was no need for him to make her a position at the tack and feed since she'd been able to get this job at the Double R. Still, Will wasn't quite yet to giving Matt Boyle the go-ahead to shoot the rest of the paperwork through on the business's change of ownership, even if Lacey had passed that particular test of her integrity. Although in putting hers through one, Will had a feeling his own character could stand a little im-proving.

But he *wasn't* Iron Will Proffitt, almighty cattle baron!

He leveled a surly stare at Lacey's slight figure. So in her opinion women had little power? Well, begging her pardon, but in his opinion they had it all. Really, here it was years later and still, with just the hint of inflection in a soft voice or the flash of a feminine eye, his ex-wife's last words and all the accompanying feelings of coming up short were brought back to him in an instant: *I need more than you can give me,*

Or was it actually nothing so general but Lacey herself who called such words up with a vividness?

Did she honestly not know what her effect was on men? he wondered ruefully as he watched her reach up to lever her end of another panel into the bed.

Muttering a terse oath, Will straightened and dragged his leather gloves out of his back pocket as he headed over to the truck, intent on putting himself out of his misery.

"Here," he said, grabbing hold of a panel and hefting it up and on top of the stack already in the truck. "We need to get a move on. It's nearly eleven and I'd like to have the chute set up so the boys can start right in after dinner gettin' that bunch of calves over on the Granger place dosed and tagged."

Lacey obligingly stepped back as Will hoisted the last panel into the truck. Yancy gave it a straightening, all the while scrutinizing his boss with a sardonic lift of his bushy eyebrows.

Yancy had known Will since forever, and he should have guessed his foreman would pick up on some of the dynamics flying around since Will hired Lacey. Of course, Yancy wasn't exactly immune to Lacey, either, because there were a lot better things he could be doing than help her load panels on a truck.

"If you're in such an all-fire hurry, boss," Yancy said, "why'n't you and Lacey grab your lunches and tea jugs and go on out to pasture while I load up the other truck with the dosing guns and taggin' equipment? Y'all can start puttin' the chute together, and I'll meet ya there soon's I can."

He turned his head to spit tobacco juice on the ground, but Will caught the hint of a smirk lurking beneath the bristle-brush mustache as the old wrangler added, "There's that little spot along the west fence line under the shade of a hackberry that makes for a right nice place to eat."

Now it was Will's turn to raise a wry eyebrow at his foreman. "Thanks for the recommendation."

Yet he couldn't dispute Yancy's logic, and so it was a few minutes later that Will found himself jolting down an old cow path behind the wheel of the cattle truck, the fence panels banging around in the bed and Lacey across the seat from him holding on to the window jamb to keep from being jarred out of her place. He downshifted in an effort to keep the teeth-rattling bumps to a minimum, and abruptly got put out with himself

78

for doing so.

Once they reached the pasture, it was relatively quick work unloading the panels and putting together the chute. Will and Lacey worked alongside each other, attaching the metal panels together with pliers and a couple of wrenches.

He slanted her a covert glance as she crouched and gave one nut a tightening twist. She'd been distant since the incident by the barn, making a point of not getting into a tit for tat with him — and could he blame her, the way he practically jumped down her throat each time he came face-to-face with her?

"So," Will said, giving a grunt as he wrung one last turn out of a nut, "am I in line to get my head chewed off if I was to ask you to elaborate on a subject?"

Lacey eyed him warily. "Like what?"

"Like women havin' to fight to keep us men from completely runnin' roughshod over you." He pocketed the wrench and fit another panel into place, concentrating a bit more than needed and taking a tad more care than usual to secure the bolt.

Finally he said, "Y'know, you're right. I can't know what that feels like, not . . . exactly, at least. But I can imagine it's not a real good feeling."

"No," she said quietly, "it isn't. It's never a good feeling to be always on your guard, not to have control of your life, to have your choices limited or cut off from you."

"Choices — to do what?"

"Anything. Everything. What to do with your life, how to live it."

"You're not tellin' me you didn't have hundreds of choices when you were a countess and had all that fame and money and power?" he asked, not twigging in to how blunt he'd been until he observed her meticulously lining up the holes on the two panels before inserting a bolt through them with more care than strictly necessary — and not answering him.

She was drawing into herself even more — protecting herself, he realized. He didn't like to think she felt she had to do so with him, but then, he'd shown about as much tact as a hick cowpoke too long out on the range and in the company of cattle.

He thought a bit longer about how to pose his next question. "So how do you handle it, then?" he asked. "Not havin' choices, that is, or feeling you don't have any control over that."

She hesitated, as if constructing her response carefully, then said, "Well, you can't let it get the better of you. You have to find some . . . some trust within yourself that's got nothing to do with size or strength or power or money, and believe that trust will help you make it through whatever trial comes your way."

Her voice fell to a whisper. "Otherwise you'd always be afraid. And no one can live their life that way."

Will chewed on the inside of his cheek. Yes, now that she mentioned it, he had seen her in some of the photos, had watched some of the news clips of her and how she'd always been surrounded by people. He could imagine it would have been hard for her to keep herself together with everyone wanting to touch the magic, wanting a piece of her to take home for their own.

Yet he still couldn't imagine why she would come back and bury herself here. She sure didn't give the impression she was pining away for the man who'd made her into a fairy tale come true, or even for the life-style she'd grown accustomed to. But surely she would have made a friend or two who might have taken her in, if only for a while, or gotten her a position doing something more along the lines of what ex-countesses did to make ends meet.

Will scratched one finger down his cheek. "What would you do if you had a choice?"

Her downturned features became more distant still, and Will wondered what he *could* ask this woman that didn't make him feel she thought his next move would be to devour her or something.

She had a piece of hay stuck to one damp cheek, and it took all his willpower to ignore it.

"How about some lunch?" he suggested, figuring *he* could do with a bit of a distraction. He headed for the truck and had taken the cooler from it and over to the shade of the hackberry before he realized Lacey was indeed anything but distant. He turned to find her standing behind him, grimly yanking her gloves off finger by finger.

"What would I do if I had a choice, instead of working here at something that's pretty much outside my capabilities and skills?" she said. "That's a real good question."

She tossed the gloves to the ground. "As you pointed out, it's not like a person in my position couldn't have learned how to do *some*thing which would qualify me for *some* kind of job *some*where!"

"Well, what did you do all day when you were a countess?" Will asked, lifting one of the jugs of tea from the cooler, twisting the cap off and handing it to her.

"I brunched or I lunched or I dined with only the most *appropriate* people." The haughty spin she put on the word didn't sound as if it'd originated with her.

"Did you not do one solitary thing of import?" He was feeling a bit freer in his phraseology than before, seeing as how she was pursuing the subject. "I mean, your entire life wasn't about consumption, conspicuous or otherwise. Was it?"

"No. I did some charity work which I found very fulfilling, even if I wasn't allowed . . . able to become involved to the degree I'd have liked to have been. You know, actually working with the people who needed me."

She took a long swig of tea and set the jar back in the cooler, a bit of business, it struck him, to keep him from spotting the vulnerability she'd done her best to hide from him.

"Do tell!" Will raised his eyebrows. "And what more could you have done for the common folk lookin' to find a minute's worth of happiness in their miserable lives than just be America's Cinderella?"

It was touch and go for a second as he wondered if he'd gone too far, or read the moment wrong.

Then he saw the spark come to her eye. "I did learn manners when I was a countess," she said, ever so dignified, "so I know how to cordially invite you to *bite me.*"

Will laughed. He couldn't help himself, and that's why, when she playfully flicked her wrist at him as if to dismiss a servant, he just as playfully caught her hand in his.

And the last of the detachment disappeared from her eyes.

It was the first time he'd seen her face completely open. Under the brim of her Western hat, her eyes were incredibly clear, their irises the green of a cottonwood at daybreak, pale but vibrant.

Even with that piece of hay still stuck to her cheek, she was a strikingly beautiful woman. She always had been: beautiful and classy in a way that had nothing to do with upbringing or noble titles.

Will realized he was staring at Lacey. The laughter had died from her eyes as she gazed up at him, her hand still in his. It was small, the bones delicate, the fingers long and slender. Of its own accord, his thumb stroked over her palm. Soft, too. He couldn't resist doing it again, holding himself very still as he did so and watching for her reaction to his advance as he would a little wild animal.

Another spark came to her eye, although this one was different. A flare, really, like the sudden shooting up of a flame from banked embers. But he also saw something akin to the fear he'd seen in her eyes that day by the barn, which near to discouraged him. Yet she didn't pull away.

A gust of cooling breeze brought with it the intermittent low of cattle and the smell of sweetgrass. He was going to end up kissing her in a second, and he had no idea how that'd go over with either of them.

Instead, Will reached up and brushed that pesky piece of hay from her cheek. When still she didn't shy away, he dared to ask the question he'd been dying to ever since she returned to Abysmal. "Why did you come back, Lacey?"

"Because I belong here," she answered forthrightly enough.

"But you'd made your choice," Will said with a lack of diplomacy he didn't care might tick her off. He wanted to know. Or maybe he had to know. "And it was to be that man's wife. It sure doesn't sound like he stinted you anything you wanted or needed."

"But you know that old saw about money not being able to buy everything?" she said. "It's true. Money and status and the security they bring aren't enough to sustain any relationship. Not even love is enough. You've got to have trust in there, on both sides. There's got to be the security of being able to trust in order to feel you *can* be vulnerable and not have that seen as a weakness to be used against you."

Her words resonated in him in a way that had nothing to do with her marriage and everything to do with his own. And pain him as it did, Will knew he had to be truthful.

"Then it sounds to me like you did what you needed to do by leavin' the marriage, Lacey," he said. "If you weren't getting what you needed. I'd say it's to your credit that you weren't willin' to settle for less than you deserved."

Clear and green and intelligent, those eyes. He didn't think he'd seen another pair like them in all his life.

"On the contrary, Will," she said, so softly he had to strain to hear her, "I still feel as if I'm at constant risk of giving my trust — and love — too easily."

Now *that* he had no clue what she meant, and he was about to ask her if perhaps the situation between her and Laslo was unfinished when something caught her attention over his shoulder. He heard the sound of an engine and knew Yancy was on his way up the track.

"Guess I better get the rest of that chute together," Lacey said.

He realized he still held her hand and let it go. She stepped back, both literally and figuratively before stooping to retrieve her gloves and pull them on, looking for all the world as if she were a queen preparing to meet her public. He almost would have done anything to bring back the fire to her eyes.

But before he could act at all, she was walking away, her slim shoulders squared and determined. And he had one thought: he was going to have to be careful and keep his little brother far, far away from her, because this was one woman whom it would be hard to meet the needs of — and hard to resist trying. And not just for Lee.

Yes, Will thought, it wasn't like him, but he'd very much made a serious tactical error.

Lacey strolled down the long, wide lane away from her parents' home. Although evening had fallen an hour ago, it was still scorching hot outside, the wind as dry as ever.

She'd had to get out of the house, though. Supper had been as silent an affair as always, at least from her mother's side of the table. Her father could be counted on to keep up a steady run of chatter, but it was difficult to make the mood seem relaxed when it was obvious it wasn't. Most of the time, Lacey could handle it, but tonight the tenseness radiating from her mother had simply gotten to her.

No, she thought, she needed to be honest: it wasn't Rachel who was getting to her. It was Will Proffitt.

She couldn't continue to work on the Double R much longer, not and keep from exhausting herself from the effort of maintaining her defenses against him. But he slipped past them so easily with his way of surprising her with his understanding.

Oh, she still didn't believe he could know entirely how she felt. Yet strangely, that didn't seem to matter so much as his wanting to understand.

What had happened to him that he might? Her father had alluded to some event a few Sundays ago, and Will himself had touched on it that first day she'd encountered him — touched on it, and immediately steered away.

What demons did he hold in check? She could barely conceive of Iron Will Proffitt having any, much less that he wouldn't have wrestled them into complete submission.

A rustle came from one of the nearby holly bushes, then a soft, "Ow!"

Lacey went ramrod straight, dread in every heartbeat. *He wouldn't have actually come here, would he?*

"Who's there?" she called with more bravado than she felt. "I'll have you know this is private property! I don't care who you are, the sheriff'll lock you up as soon as I give the order!"

"No! I'll come out. My daddy would kill me if I got 'rested!"

A slight form rose from the bushes and stepped into the beam coming from a nearby streetlight.

Lacey stared in amazement at the teen-aged girl standing before her. She was dressed in the mode of every other teen-aged girl in the Panhandle, meaning she wore a T-shirt, faded Wranglers, and scuffed roper boots. She had a Western hat on her head — and a duffel bag in her hand.

She's running away, Lacey thought with a flash of cognition. Or at least, that had been her prior intent. Right now, however, her gaze was locked like a magnet onto Lacey, without much sign of letting go.

Lacey knew that look — one of fascination, reverence and hope. She'd encountered it a dozen times in the past few weeks from girls aged five on up. Girls who'd never seen a real live Cinderella before — not only that, but a Cinderella who'd once been like them, from little bitty Abysmal, Texas. It made the fairy tale that much more real to them.

Yes, Lacey thought, she had been one of these girls once, with shining dreams and hopes. Such dreams seemed to get dreamed a whole lot more often in towns like this.

Her expectant look dimmed at Lacey's pensive gaze.

"You don't know me, do you?" she said flatly. She ducked her head, fingering her hair back behind one shoulder. "O'course, I was just a kid when you left Abysmal. I know you, though. I can't believe I'm actually standin' here with America's Cinderella!"

For once, Lacey didn't chafe at the nickname. It had been purely accidental that she had wandered out this way this evening. So what had the teenager hoped to find by coming to her house?

And then there was that duffel bag.

Lacey's curiosity — and concern — were piqued. She couldn't help but respond.

Kindly, she said, "I'm sorry, I don't remember you . . . ?"

"Jenna. Jenna Barlow. And it's okay,

Lacey." Confusion crossed her features. "It's all right if I call you Lacey, isn't it? Or Countess Lacey? I don't want to be improper or the like."

"Lacey's fine," Lacey answered, trying not to wince. She started back up the lane again, indicating Jenna could join her. "I was just taking a walk. Ever had one of those times when you just had to get out of the house or go crazy?"

"Have I ever!" Jenna said with feeling. Except Lacey could tell from the way the girl now stared at the mansion that she couldn't imagine not wanting to live in such luxury — and was looking for Lacey's secret on how to get there herself.

"How old are you, Jenna?" she asked abruptly.

"I'm seventeen. But I'll be eighteen in a few weeks."

Eighteen! The age seemed eons ago. "And then?"

The girl shot her a curious look. "That's kinda why I came here tonight, sorta to get up the courage. I don't want to stay here, that's for sure."

So she'd been right. "Why not?" Lacey asked gently.

"What would I do?" she said. "My cousin — Carla Hayes? — she lit out from here six

91

months ago herself. She's in Houston now, and she says there're lots of opportunities for girls like us there. In fact, she's got a boyfriend who works at one of the oil companies, and since he moved in and started helpin' payin' the rent, she's been able to put a down payment on a brand-new car."

She said the last as if it were too fantastic to be true.

"What about college, Jenna?" Lacey asked rather urgently. "Have you thought about college?"

She slowed in her tracks as if coming up against a roadblock. "No. Daddy says I've gotta do somethin'. He says now that I'm grown it's time I earned my keep, 'specially if I want to keep livin' in his house. But I'd rather get away like you did and meet someone who could give me everything."

Lacey tried a quivering smile. "Look, Jenna. It's not that easy. If Prince Charming was real, would I be back here in Abysmal, plain old Lacey McCoy again?"

The girl pursed her mouth, then admitted, "I guess not. But what have I got to lose by tryin'? What's to stay here for? I could leave tonight and never look back. Carla said even if I didn't find a job and a place to live right away, her boyfriend said

92

it was okay if I lived with them till I did."

Lacey swallowed back another protest. She was getting the sick feeling that there was nothing she could say which would detour Jenna from this road she was on.

"Look, Jenna," Lacey said, reaching out for her arm, drawing strength from the contact, "don't leave Abysmal without talking to me again, all right?"

Her features grew obstinate. "Why not?"

"I don't know what I might come up with for you to do here, but would you please give me some time to take a look around town and see?"

Jenna's face lit up. "You'd do that for me?"

It was then Lacey realized something about the girl: she wasn't used to having someone take a special interest in her and care about what she wanted.

"Of course, I would — and more," she answered warmly.

Lacey glanced up and saw they'd reached the front door of her parents' home. Both she and Jenna stood there for a moment, gazing up at it, the girl in rapt admiration, Lacey with mild revulsion.

Its brick facade was stark and flat, its crenelated windows set at precise intervals both upstairs and down, making it look like a dormitory. Her father wasn't so very far off the mark when he said it would make a better boardinghouse than a private home. Or one of those straitlaced, pinched-nosed English boarding schools where only the most sacred of subjects were studied, Latin and the like. Nothing useful, of course. Nothing that would send a young person out into the world with the kind of skills she could use to make her own way . . .

Lacey stared at the cold, imposing fortress of a house as realization buffeted her like a blast of the hot, dry West Texas wind.

"So what if," she murmured as if in a trance, "what if we made it into a school? No . . . no, not a school — I'd need a teaching degree. But maybe a . . . a resource center. For girls."

"What?" Jenna asked.

Lacey beamed at her, and the way the girl gazed back at her made her think she indeed looked like a candidate for Bedlam.

"Jenna, what if there was a place here in town where girls in the surrounding area, girls as young as ten or eleven all the way up to your age, could come to broaden their horizons — explore different career options — and life choices."

Choices that would provide them with the kinds of dreams that bore real fruit by helping them to realize their potential as proud, independent, self-confident and capable young women. And any man who came along would have to play catch-up to meet them on equal ground.

Lacey's mind whirled, thoughts whipping about so fast she could scarce grasp them on the way by: her father could teach the girls home and auto repair; he'd adore it. Lee had mentioned to her recently he'd become somewhat of a whiz at navigating the Internet and its own world of possibilities. She herself would relish researching all sorts of topics for discussion on life choices. As for Mother — Lacey's euphoria dipped. Her mother would be a hard sell, to put it mildly. And the home was still her parents' — not hers. Not only that, but starting a resource center would mean an outflow of money, not an inflow, especially since Lacey knew right now she wouldn't charge any of the girls for coming.

Which didn't do much to solve the problem of how to make ends meet.

And yet . . . even if it needed some of the kinks worked out, the idea was a good one, a worthy one. One Lacey could get behind with all her heart and make her own. *Be* her own self, and show that to not only these girls but to everyone else. And wasn't that what *she* needed, more than anything else on earth?

She didn't know how it would all come about, but she needed to trust that the way to proceed would present itself along the way. But she must take that first step.

"A resource center for girls?" Jenna asked, bringing Lacey back to front and center.

"Yes! But I'd need help. *Your* help, Jenna, especially as someone the younger girls looked up to and would follow. And I'd pay you as an employee, too."

Jenna's face was a study in suspicion, pride, doubt — and hope. Hope was definitely there, though.

"Sure," she said with a nonchalant shrug that didn't fool Lacey a bit. "I guess I could help."

Lacey couldn't stop herself; she caught Jenna in a spontaneous hug of her own uncontainable hope. She felt like Scarlett O'Hara must have at the moment when she laid her cheek against those green velvet drapes and realized it was within her power to save her home.

The difference was, Lacey hoped to save something much more valuable, much more precious: the future for girls like Jenna.

And maybe in the process, she would seize her own as well.

CHAPTER FIVE

Lee and Hank were having a fine time of it.

Coming into the living room, pitcher of lemonade in hand, Lacey found Lee apprising her father of the differences between a mouse and a touch pad, while Hank instructed the younger man on how to ground the outlets for the computers which would go in the room. She couldn't help but see it as a sign of the cooperative spirit — and support — which would make her undertaking a success.

She still had a lot of work in front of her. In the past week, she had mostly used her father and Lee to help rearrange furniture into more of a classroom setting, and was just now getting to modifying the rooms for their specific uses. Jenna had been a boon, too, with her boundless energy.

Lacey had also contacted an antique dealer in Dallas who'd been more than willing to come and take a look at the pieces which would be sold, the money to be applied toward the computers and other equipment. She'd visited the library in Amarillo to check out books on starting a nonprofit organization, and had sent in her application to obtain status as one. She'd also gone to the Abysmal State Bank and gotten an application for start-up financing, with the house as collateral, to use until she'd had a chance to raise money through grants and donations, and to the city hall for a permit to run a business in a residential area. She hoped to hear back any day now on both.

For then her resource center would be official. At the thought, Lacey found herself terrified and exhilarated at once. She was making a real dream come true.

Of course, Mother had balked at first. But she'd had to admit in the end there wasn't much to be gained by preserving this mausoleum as it was, even if the resource center didn't succeed.

But it would, Lacey vowed. It had to.

"Who could use a glass of lemonade?" she asked.

Both men looked up with the same expression of interest. "Don't mind if I do," Hank said, reaching for a glass.

"Sounds good," Lee agreed.

It occurred to Lacey as she watched them down their lemonade in gulps that these two were so alike in temperament they could have been father and son. Both were forthright men who dealt with people straight on and didn't require a lot of figuring out.

She wondered how Will had gotten to be such an uptight, opinionated . . . enigma.

She hadn't seen him since she went into his office to give notice. He'd been characteristically tight-lipped as she'd explained how she had never been suited to the job on the Double R, and how now that he didn't have to worry she was going to take a job from Lee, the reason for her working for him was moot.

But she didn't tell Will about her resource center.

It wasn't as if he wouldn't find out. Satellite communications had nothing on Abysmal's grapevine. But because of its personal significance, her venture made her vulnerable. She simply wasn't ready to put it out there for Abysmal — and especially Will Proffitt — to come and take a peek at it.

She set the pitcher on a nearby table. "I'll just leave the rest of the lemonade here for seconds," she told Lee and Hank, and winced as she turned to go.

"You all right, darlin'?" her father asked.

"Yes." Leaning a hand on the table, Lacey slid her boot off and massaged her foot. "I think these ropers were intended for looks, not going up and down those stairs a hundred times a day. I'll be fine. Nothing a hot bath won't fix later."

"Whyn't you leave off early and go hop into that fancy Jacuzzi outside?" Hank suggested.

Didn't that sound heavenly! Lacey thought regretfully. She'd already given Jenna the rest of the afternoon off.

"But, Daddy, Lee's been taking off from the tack and feed each afternoon specifically to help out, and I wouldn't feel right about not doing my part."

"Shoot, you've both been workin' like dogs." He glanced at Lee, who'd risen with a prodigious cracking of joints. "Go on and join her, kid. You look like you could use a hot soak, too. You can wear the pair of trunks Rachel bought me when we first moved in here. Don't think I've worn 'em but twice."

"I'd be obliged," Lee responded, obviously needing no coaxing. He must have seen she still needed convincing, though. "Come on, Lacey. It'll be like old times. Remember how you used to be a fool to swim in the stock tank on the Double R?"

Lacey grinned. She had indeed used to beg Lee to sneak her out to the stock tank to find some relief from the incessant heat. "All right. I guess someone may as well get some use out of that cement pond in the backyard."

Ten minutes later Lacey slid into the hot, frothing water with a half sigh, half moan. Lee had already made himself at home, arms resting outstretched along the Jacuzzi's tiled edge, the brim of his Stetson covering his face down to his nose.

Yes, Lee was every bit a loose-walking, slow-talking, live-and-let-living, hard-loving cowboy. Right then he seemed the dead opposite of Will. The thought made her sober. She'd been meaning to ask Lee something, and now seemed as good a time as any to bring the subject up.

"I was wondering, Lee. Did something happen? With you, I mean." She shaded her eyes against the setting sun. "I've gotten the impression from a couple of people it had to do with me."

He didn't say anything for a few minutes, and Lacey wondered if she would again be left in the dark, when Lee lifted the brim of his hat with one finger and peered at her from beneath it, a look of chagrin on his face.

"I'd wondered if you knew," he said on an embarrassed laugh. "I guess you've got a right to know the whole story. Might explain a few things about me — and Will."

Now she was *really* curious. "Lee Proffitt, you tell me right now what happened here while I was gone!"

"Don't get your back sulled up," he said good-naturedly. But he made a bit of a production of lifting his hat and setting it back square on his head as he sat up straight.

"It was actually what happened when we got word back here that you were all set to marry Nicolai Laslo. Y'see, we'd barely had time to absorb the news when this buncha media folk came around lookin' for stories about you, especially what kind of kid you'd been, anything they could hang a fresh angle on. You know what I'm talking about."

She nodded. Unfortunately, she did.

"Then when they ran out of those stories," Lee continued, "they started diggin'. Asking about old boyfriends, of which there was me. They surrounded me like a swarm of fire ants, askin' what it was like to've been sweethearts with America's Cinderella. One wanted to know what it felt like to have gotten kissed by you and stayed a frog!"

Lacey put a hand to her mouth. "Lee, I'm

so sorry! I can't believe you had to go through that just for having dated me!"

"Well, it was partially my fault," he admitted, throwing her another of those abashed glances. "See, I'd been poppin' off at the mouth for months about how you were gonna come back from Europe — and we were gonna tie the knot ourselves."

Her breath left her in a whoosh of air. "But . . . but, Lee, did I ever give you the impression we were going to be married?"

"No, Lacey, not once." He stretched an arm out and squeezed one hand as she clutched her drawn-up knees. "I was able to appreciate that fact later, but at the time . . . well, at the time I was howlin'-at-the-moon crazy in love with you."

Lacey didn't realize her mouth had dropped open until Lee leaned toward her with a tolerant smile and gave it a nudge shut.

"I didn't know," she said, mortified. "I mean, I know everyone thought we were sweethearts, but we used to laugh at that, remember?"

Simply thinking about it now brought a smile to her face. But her smile died at Lee's bemused expression. "You only laughed because I did, didn't you?" Lacey asked.

He gave a shrug, then nodded. "It wasn't

your fault, Lacey. I was ripe as a cow chip to get my heart hung up on some girl, and if it hadn't've been you, it would have been some other sweet young thing. But I didn't see that then."

She didn't entirely believe him. He was such a dear man. A dear friend, then and now. She asked gently, "What did you do?"

"What else could I do?" Water sluicing off of him, he hoisted himself up to sit on the edge of the Jacuzzi. "I faced the music — or the reporters, as it were — and admitted we hadn't been anything but friends. Thankfully everyone in Abysmal backed up my story, even when they knew different. I'll never forget their support — that and how not a word has been said since in this town about the situation."

Arms locked at the elbow on either side of him, he stared into the bubbling water. "I have Will to thank for that. And more, because a week or so after the reporters lost interest and left, I worked myself into a blue lonesome and took off without a word. Will found me I don't know how many days later."

Lee heaved a sigh. "I think up to then Will thought I didn't have anything more wrong with me than a rash of foolishness. But that scared him. I don't know that it didn't scare me, too."

Lacey put her hand out over his, and he gave her a rueful look. "At least now you can understand why Will's been protective of me, and why I allow it, to a point. Like him giving you a job on the Double R so I wouldn't hire you."

"You knew what he was doing?" she asked, surprised.

"Oh, sure." A certain gleam entered his eye. "But I think the time's come for him to learn a thing or two about Kid Brother taking care of himself. I mean, we've never talked about it, but I know he pretty much engineered the whole situation those years ago to keep the lid on my predicament."

Naturally he would, Lacey thought. Will Proffitt reigned in this town. Yet if Will had used his influence to help his brother, then she was grateful to him.

"What about Will?" Lacey asked abruptly.

"What about him?" Lee asked back.

"I get the impression something happened to him, too. Something . . . that hurt him, too."

Lee's scrutiny was penetrating. She avoided it by boosting herself up next to him. It was awfully hot out here in the sun, she noticed of a sudden.

"I'm not asking just for curiosity's sake,

you know," she defended herself in a tart voice.

"Well, if not for curiosity's sake, then why?"

"Just . . . just . . . oh, never mind." To pursue the subject now seemed foolhardy, although she *was* dying of curiosity. But maybe the entire town had taken another oath of silence, this one on the subject of Will Proffitt.

The thought brought her back around to the subject at hand. "Does it hurt still, Lee?" she asked softly.

He shrugged. "No more'n the heartburn I get after I've had a bowl of chili down at the café."

But somehow she knew it did still hurt. Impulsively, Lacey leaned to the side and gave Lee a kiss of thanks on the cheek, very schoolgirlish and innocent. And there was nothing wrong with feeling those feelings for him, she thought. Especially when Lee broke out in his aw-shucks smile and put an arm around her in one of his old, affection-ate hugs, which she enjoyed immensely for the reassurance it gave her in simply being free to feel such honest emotions again.

Until she looked over Lee's shoulder to see Will standing half a dozen feet away with a thunderous look in his gray eyes. And it was leveled straight at her.

At the sight, all the doubt, qualms and misgivings Lacey had briefly hoped herself shed of at last sprang up in her like a house afire.

This is it, Will thought.

He had always held a secret suspicion — or dread — that the tight control he kept over himself came with a price, meaning there were certain inciting incidents waiting to happen which would inevitably act like a match to the fuse on his powder keg of restraint. Normally, he could detect such situations in the making and take action to defuse them or himself. But the sight of his brother with his arm around Lacey — skin all rosy and dewy and her looking nine-tenths to a million bucks in that pale-yellow bathing suit — was not one of those times.

"What is goin' on here?" Will asked, not realizing until the words were out of his mouth how he sounded like a stern father — or a jealous boyfriend. Strangely, he *did* feel betrayed, although not by his own brother, but by Lacey.

Her gaze certainly held an element of trepidation, which Will had come to despise himself for arousing in her.

With all his might, he tried to moderate

his reaction. But the lid on his temper gave another threatening rumble as his brother not only kept his arm around Lacey but dropped his hand to her waist and gave it a chummy squeeze, all with the same innocent look with which a five-year-old Lee had given his older brother while pouring maple syrup into Will's good boots.

To her credit, Lacey tried prying his fingers off her ribs, but Lee was having none of it. "Goin' on?" he asked blandly. "Why, nothing's goin' on, Will."

"Oh, that's abundantly obvious, believe me. Yancy and I came into town to do some business and thought we'd stop in at the tack and feed to see how my kid brother's doing. But wouldn't you know, Jimmy Ray says you haven't seen four o'clock around the store for the past week. Says you head for here each day to 'help out' Lacey McCoy."

He'd been so angry at hearing that he'd instructed Yancy to go on without him while he walked over here so as to find a little perspective — an apparently pointless ambition, because he was even more aggravated.

"So what if I take off early? It's my business to run how I see fit, isn't it — or is it?" Lee asked pointedly.

"We'll see about that, won't we?" Will

retorted with as barbed an emphasis.

At least that got Lee to drop his arm from around Lacey's waist so he could rise to his feet. "And just what's that supposed to mean?"

"It means you've still got some provin' to do, and this episode today has sure enough set you back a spell."

Lee's features flushed with anger and he actually took a step toward Will. "Not if I've got anything to say about it!"

"Stop it now!" Lacey interjected, scrambling to her feet as well. "I won't have you two scrapping in my backyard like a couple of rowdy cowboys!"

"Right," Will agreed. "Come on, Lee, let's leave the lady here to the important matter of gettin' a tan. Unless, of course, your idea of 'helping out' includes your own pursuit of such shallow concerns, in which case I'd be glad to wait while you go on toastin' your backside."

Lee's jaw bulged with his restraint. "I'm ready right now," he said evenly.

"Ready for one of those rodeo beefcake calendars, you mean?"

Lee seemed to remember only then he was dressed in nothing but a pair of trunks and his Stetson. "Fine! My clothes are over in that thing called a cabana, if you can hold your horses one minute while I change."

Will watched him stalk off before turning back to Lacey.

She looked like a daffodil, golden and perfect. Make that one indignant daffodil. Fists clenched at her sides, chest rising and falling with her wrath, she looked set to go off like a case of fireworks herself.

Boy, but the fire in her eyes was a powerful temptation to him! It was all he could do not to kiss her, just to witness the flame shoot higher.

Funny, but right then his mood changed from rankled to chipper, just like that.

"Don't you dare come down on Lee for being here and helpin' me!" she snapped.

"Actually, he looked like he was helping himself." Will raised his eyebrows. "Or was that the plan?"

Her green eyes sparked. "You don't know a thing about what's going on!"

"Then why don't you enlighten me? I'm all ears."

She opened her mouth, ready to answer him, but something stopped her. Of a sudden, the wariness returned to her eyes, that drawing back and closing off to protect herself, and he got nettled all over again that she did.

Lee came out of the cabana, shirttails

dangling and boots in hand. He gave a polite nod of goodbye to Lacey. "Thanks for the hot tub. I'll see you tomorrow, same time as always."

The last was obviously said for Will's benefit. Lee spared him not a glance but stalked past him as if he didn't exist. The effect was completely spoiled by the soles of his bare feet making contact with the hot brick decking around the pool, so he had to hop-skip his way to the grass on the front lawn.

Will gave a parting nod of his own to Lacey before striding to Lee's dually pickup parked in the drive. He got in the driver's side and held his hand out the window for the keys.

Lee's chin jutted obstinately.

"Just give 'em to me," Will said mildly. "Your driving's bound to be erratic since you've got your shorts in a twist."

His brother didn't say anything, just dug into his jeans pocket and slammed the keys into Will's palm. He got into the passenger side, yanked on his socks, and shoved his feet into his boots, all without a word.

When they were out on the road and halfway home with the air still thick as mud in the cab, Will decided he'd better get this out and over with.

"Look, Lee, I'm not tryin' to run your life. But you gotta see you can't go on neglecting the tack and feed."

"For your information, I'm *not* neglectin' the tack and feed!" Lee reached into the back seat of the extended cab and pulled out a manila file, which he waved in Will's face. "Have you taken a look at the month-end numbers, Will? Have you?"

"Of course I've looked at the numbers!" Will said, tight-lipped.

"Then you'll know the business is doin' just fine! I've not just met projection but I've bettered it six months in a row."

It was true; in the nine months he'd managed the store, Lee had been keeping up a steady growth with relatively minor setbacks and adjustments.

When Will said nothing, Lee tossed the folder on the seat between them. "I should have known you wouldn't give me credit."

Will's fingers clenched on the steering wheel but he kept up the poker face. "That's because now's the time when you need most to keep up your momentum — take a look at what's selling and what's not, make changes to inventory."

"But *I* think now's the perfect time for me to start implementing some of those management techniques you sent me to U.T. to learn." He set his hat on his knee and pulled a comb out of his back pocket. "I mean, you're the one who said I'd need real soon to train Jimmy Ray on how to hold down the store so the place would still get run if I was sick or took vacation."

Pausing in combing his hair back, Lee shot him a keen glance. "And while we're on the subject, have you done the same at the Double R, dividing up your responsibilities and settling each on different people?"

"Oh, for the love of . . . of course I have!" Kid Brother was beginning to tick him off. "It wouldn't be fair to the men and their families who depend on the Double R continuing not to have every aspect of the operation backed up."

"But do you *know* the place could go on without you?" Lee persisted. "Because let's face it, Will, you haven't taken a day off in the past ten years!"

Will slammed on the brakes and shoved the gearshift into park before turning to his brother with a cutting glare. Lee's eyes shot daggers right back at Will. "And I won't get to in the next ten if you keep up your habits of givin' away your time and energy like they're batches of biscuits you can just go into the kitchen and whip up more of!"

"That's it." Lee thrust open the pickup's

door and headed around the front of the truck. Will was out of his seat in a split second so as to meet him halfway. They squared off right there in the middle of the road.

"Why can't you just admit I'm doing a bang-up job with the tack and feed and it's high time you turned ownership of it over to me?" Lee charged. "You think I don't know what you're doin' with Matt Boyle? He hasn't been able to look me in the eye for the past month!"

His mouth twisted in disgust. "I always suspected you were an A-1 certified jerk, Will, but now I find myself clearing up all doubt."

Will took that one on the chin without a flinch. "Let's just say I'm through with pickin' up the pieces of your life."

"Oh, that's right, I forgot. I can't be trusted to run my own, 'cause everyone knows Lee Proffitt is just like his daddy!"

"Well, you are! You just let people walk all over you, Lacey McCoy most of all!"

"So that's what this is about." Lee's stance went rigid, his hands curling into fists, but he didn't raise them. Instead he let fire with a different kind of salvo. "Well, I'd rather be a doormat ten times over than like you — because you're nothin' but a control freak

114

who could probably never let go of your iron control long enough to find out what it is a woman really needs!"

Will moved not a muscle. Lee put up his dukes anyway, set to spring into action at the flick of an eyelash.

It had been eight years since brother had raised arms against brother. Will knew it was that long because he remembered exactly the circumstances of when and why Lee had, which were a few months after Will had hauled him back from El Paso. Lee had been moping around for weeks, and Will had had enough. The kid had come at him with both fists flying when Will told him he could finish the job he'd started in El Paso any number of ways, just let Will know how he wanted the Countess Laslo to be informed — telegram, phone, or maybe just let her see the photos in the newspapers, since every tabloid on earth would be clamoring for the story of the poor, dumb sot of a cowboy who ate his heart out for a woman.

Sure, he'd been and still was a jerk about the matter! If anyone would die for love it'd be Lee, and the obsession his brother had for Lacey had scared Will — enough so that when his own heartbreak had hit the fan, he'd remembered his fear for Lee and had held in his pain.

Held it in — and was still holding it in.

That's where the brothers differed, for although Will had gone on with life without a pause, inside he'd cratered as deeply as any man ever brought to his knees by love. And now, looking at Lee, Will wasn't sure his younger brother hadn't come out the better for letting it all hang out and getting his heartbreak out of his system.

And maybe that's what Lee was trying to do for him — that is, if Will would let him . . . let him do a lot of things.

"You're right, Lee," Will said abruptly.

Lee's fists dropped like dead weights. "What?"

"You're right. I haven't been fair to you with the tack and feed. About a lot of things. And I apologize for that. I need to step back and give you full control of your business." He squinted at the horizon, shimmering with heat, beyond which lay his ranch — his and Lee's. "And . . . and I'd like you to take more of a hand in runnin' the Double R."

Lee looked completely flummoxed. "You'd let me carry some of the responsibility for the ranch?"

Will shrugged. "Sure. I *have* worked hard to make that ranch into something, and the last thing I want is for it to go down the drain should something happen to me."

Lee set a boot on the immaculate chrome bumper of his truck, a sure sign he was moved by Will's offer. "I'd really like that, Will. I've always had an interest in ranching. Actually felt I might have a certain knack for it, given a chance. But there was always Big Brother who knew best."

Will acknowledged his complicity in that perception with a nod. "Well, then, whenever you get Jimmy Ray trained up to be able to hold down the store for you, you're welcome to start easin' into some of the management on the Double R."

A wry smile tugged at his mouth. "Who knows but you might discover you got a little of the Proffitt control freak in you yourself."

"Oh, help me!" Lee said with a groan.

They laughed together, which brought a warmth to Will's insides. But he knew they needed to settle a certain matter before they could become true partners.

"I gotta know one thing first, Lee." He worked his mouth around the words for a minute, then decided to just come on out with them. "Are you still in love with Lacey McCoy?"

His brother cocked his head as if listening

real hard, and Will added hastily, "I'm just askin' because I need to know, businesswise, if you're gonna go through another killer heartbreak when she drops you cold."

"Boy, would somebody get this man a bran muffin?" Lee begged the sky above before dropping his gaze back to Will. "Just what makes you so all-fire certain Lacey's gettin' ready to throw me out like yesterday's newspaper?"

Avoiding his brother's eyes, Will dropped to his haunches and made a production out of tracing the Double R brand over and over in the dirt.

What made him think that? Will knew, and it was because he'd have to be stone cold dead not to pick up on the vibrations between Lacey — and himself.

He didn't entirely know what they were about, especially given how she tended to bring out the worst in him. Or maybe the bigger question was, what exactly was it he brought out in her?

He'd sure done a lot of thinking about it in the past few weeks, and he had just about figured that part out: Lacey saw him as a threat, which was why she got all queenly on him and as verbose as a revival preacher.

Now, a threat to what in particular — that was still a poser. It was more than a matter of physical dominance or power; it seemed something a lot more elemental.

A snippet of dialogue came back to Will, something about love not being enough. Trust, Lacey had said, was the key in a relationship, so both parties could be vulnerable. That's what he'd seen her be today with his brother. And maybe that was because Lee had been the same with her.

Suddenly, Will wanted her to be like that with him, to trust him so. The yearning engulfed him like the devil's own fire.

Just as quickly, he summoned all of his will to screw the hatch down on such a longing. Because wanting her to trust him surely meant he would have to open up and trust her, too. Call him a control freak, but he wasn't willing to let go. Not yet.

But Will was honest enough with himself to admit he wasn't about to let go either of the memory of Lacey's small hand in his, or the way her eyes had widened then flared at his touch.

Will looked up at his brother. "Look, Lee, I'm not sayin' Lacey *will* give you another case of the lonely onlies, but you don't exactly have a stellar track record in that department, you know."

Lee's returning gaze was both tolerant and exasperated. "Oh, all right. To answer your questions, no, I'm not gonna get my needle stuck again on some somebody-done-somebody-wrong song — at least not with Lacey. So you can quit being all up in arms with her for that and just admit to what you really are bent out of shape with her about."

He hooked his thumbs in his belt loops. " 'Cause I'm tellin' you right now, Big Brother, if you want to know the Proffitt you need to worry about fallin' in love with Lacey McCoy, I'm lookin' at him."

With that, he brushed past Will as he crossed to the driver's side of his truck and got in. Will rose slowly to find Lee grinning at him through the windshield as he cranked the ignition and gunned the engine.

"You better get on in here unless you want to get run over," he said out the window.

Now there's an idea, Will thought. Might be the only way to save himself a whole lot of trouble. And heartache.

CHAPTER SIX

Lacey felt like a prize heifer on display at the county fair.

People had been filing past her for half an hour, some merely congenial, some mildly curious. But most were excruciatingly fawning. And all anxious beyond measure that they get the opportunity to have a brief "audience" with her.

Because when again would Abysmal's Summer Fling — the gussied-up name her mother's ladies' group had come up with for what was basically an evening of good old Texas barbecue, awful-tasting punch and two-stepping — be graced with the presence of a bona fide ex-countess?

And the worst of it was, her mother had been standing at her side the entire time, her features positively glowing. Lacey hadn't seen her so happy in years.

For tonight, at least, the glass slipper still fit, midnight was hours away, and her daughter was still America's Cinderella.

Lacey supposed it was a small sacrifice, really, in the scheme of things. Not feeling much like socializing these days, either as the ex-countess or simple Lacey McCoy, she wouldn't have come tonight except for her mother's pleas.

She'd learned two days ago that her start-up financing hadn't been approved, which was a somewhat disappointing blow. She'd pumped herself back up again by reminding herself she could always go out of town for financing. Except then she'd received word from city hall that her application for a business license had been denied.

The news still held the power to deflate whatever optimism she'd breathed into her hopes. But the cold hard fact which kept staring her in the face was that if she couldn't get a business license, then she'd be violating zoning restrictions to set up her resource center.

And wouldn't you know, Matt Boyle, the lending officer at the bank, and the mayor, Dale Willis, were both here and of a cheerful bearing.

She couldn't help but take it personally.

It simply wasn't fair! She'd asked them why she'd been turned down and both had been vague — and downright disapproving in a "don't you worry your pretty head, little lady" way. And wasn't that the way the story had gone since time immemorial? Cinderella didn't take matters into her own hands but waited patiently for some big, strong Prince Charming to come along and save the day. Because heaven forbid she'd be capable of taking care of herself!

Well, she no longer had the time or patience or especially the desire to play that game again.

Lacey could only hope Jenna, standing on the other side of the hall with her friends, didn't catch the byplay that was taking place this evening, with her being treated like a princess. She had spent too much time with the teenager establishing herself as plain old Lacey McCoy.

She felt a squeeze to her elbow.

"Matt Boyle is headin' this way," her mother whispered.

"So?"

"I want you to be nice to him."

"Oh, I'll be as nice as he's been to me, I assure you," Lacey said out of the corner of her mouth.

"Lacey, please. You know what it's like to live in this town, and makin' enemies of the people who have influence is not going to do anyone any good."

Her mother was right. Lacey may have gotten turned down, but she still needed people like Matt on her side if she was going to make a go of her resource center. It didn't make her feel any better about it, however.

"Hey there, Lacey."

She swung around to find Matt Boyle close beside her, his hat, weekend-cowboy new, tipped back on his head and a cocky air about him which almost drowned out the pungent cologne he wore.

"Hello, Matt," she said, trying not to begrudge him every degree of warmth in her voice.

There was an awkward silence Lacey felt no compunction to help fill before he finally piped up. "Fine social the ladies have put together here, don't you think?"

"Absolutely."

Another interminable pause.

"You're lookin' especially fetching tonight," Matt said.

Fighting off the urge to bat her eyelashes and coo a simpering, "Why, you unmerciful flatterer! You're just tryin' to break my li'l ol' heart!" Lacey instead answered, "Thank you."

Matt apparently found nothing lacking in

the enthusiasm of her response, for he then said with the same good ol' boy bravado, "You know, I've been thinkin' we oughta hook up together."

"You mean date?" she asked, even though she'd seen this one coming from a mile away.

"Well, yeah. I mean, I heard it around town you've been seein' Lee Proffitt again, but I thought, why not throw my hat into the ring, too, especially when I've got just as much to offer you."

Lacey had an urge to ream her ear out with her little finger. "I beg your pardon?"

"Well, I *am* a vice president at the bank," he said expansively. "You can't get much more security than that, and there's no guarantee Lee'll make a go of that tack and feed in the long run, if you know what I mean."

"I'm sure I don't," Lacey said as frostily as any royal who ever graced a throne. Unless . . . A suspicion snapped on in her head like a neon light. "This whole come-on wouldn't have anything to do with me getting turned down for financing, would it? You know, thickening the plot so you can enter stage left and untie Nell from the railroad tracks. *Would it?*"

Matt's mouth fell open. "It wasn't like

that," he protested. "I mean, even given the collateral of your parents' house, you couldn't show a definite income from the center. The bank isn't in the business of funding gambles of that size."

"But my parents have been law-abiding, upstanding citizens of Abysmal for thirty years! Did you seriously doubt they — or I — couldn't make good on the loan?"

Matt's round face turned as red as a tomato, and the perspiration sprang out on his forehead. Well, she was a little steamed herself. "It was a judgment call —"

"And who was the judge?"

He at least had the grace to look ashamed. "Really, Lacey, I don't normally pull strings —"

"But you couldn't resist this time, and why should you? I'm pretty much fair game at this point, not to mention in dire need of being saved from myself. Because it seems everyone in this town knows what's best for me but me!"

That terrible chain around her throat wrenched tighter, like that on a rack, and nearly overwhelmed her. She wished for her father's sturdy presence right then, desperately, or even Lee's. No — how she could make such wishes when she was fighting at

126

this very moment to keep from being rescued?

But rescuing wasn't what she wanted! She just needed someone right now to be on her side. And was there no one in the world who could be here for her? No one at all?

Now there was a storm brewing if he'd ever seen one.

Will watched the little scene unfold on the other side of the assembly hall. Matt Boyle had hitched up his britches a good ten times, which meant he was getting up the gumption to approach the lady focused in his amorous sights.

Will didn't need a script to know what was going on. Matt was so obvious about his intent that both Lacey and her mother would have had to have been blindfolded not to see him coming. And from the look on Lacey's face, this guy not only didn't have a chance, he was in for one big-time spurning.

Will grinned.

Then Lacey's mother leaned toward her to say something, her face the picture of patience, as if she were explaining simple arithmetic to a kindergartner. Lacey murmured something back, short and sweet, which made Rachel McCoy huff another

127

comment of some kind. Lacey got an obstinate look on her face but obviously took her mother's warning to heart, for she said no more.

That's when Matt made his move. He bobbed out a greeting, which Lacey barely acknowledged. He made another attempt. Again, no luck.

He looked like an ungainly bumblebee buzzing around an exquisite rosebud, without a clue how to get inside.

"No mystery Boyle's staking out his claim 'fore anyone else does, ain't it?" Dumas Findley said beside him.

"He's sure enough givin' it the old high school try."

"Best entertainment to be had till the band gets a-goin'," Dumas remarked. "Say, ain't that your brother just got here?"

Will turned in the direction of Dumas' nod. Lee was indeed making his way into the hall, greeting a few buddies with slaps on their backs, shaking the hand of a few more, tipping his hat to the ladies. "Yup."

"Well, now, correct me if I'm wrong, but hasn't *he* been keepin' company with Lacey?"

"They're friends, that's all," Will answered tersely.

He turned his attention back to Lacey and

Matt. Something must have happened when he looked away, because Lacey's face had gone slack, and her eyes had glazed over in shock.

She said something to Matt, who actually raised his hands, the universal language for backing off, but she came at him anyway. The volume of her voice rose, but Will still couldn't understand what she was saying. It was enough to turn a few heads in their direction, though. Murmurs of curiosity carried like a wave over the heads of the throng.

Will saw the instant his brother marked the situation with Lacey. He started shouldering his way through the crowd.

"Hoo boy, this is gonna be good!" Dumas rubbed his hands together. "I ain't seen a good fight since I left the rodeo. My money's on Lee, that's for sure. Boyle may've been one tough linebacker, but he's soft as a cupcake nowadays."

But Will barely heard Dumas, for next he saw Lacey slump, as if a yoke with two fifty-pound sandbags on either end had been placed across her shoulders. It was like looking at pure-D discouragement, without the additives.

He'd seen her distant, he'd seen her raring mad, he'd seen her wary as a cat. But he'd never seen her defeated.

In the next instant Will, too, was cutting through the crowd toward Lacey. He wasn't sure why, but he wanted to reach her before Lee did.

They crossed paths just short of Matt and Lacey. Lee's eyes widened at the sight of him and his obvious intent.

"I've got the situation covered," Will said in a tone that brooked no argument.

"Whatever you say, Big Brother," Lee said with a grin.

Over Lacey's shoulder, Will threw Matt Boyle a warning glance that made the younger man's face blanch. She must have sensed something was in the offing because when he touched her arm, she whirled around as if expecting to defend her life. He realized he'd caught her off guard, utterly exposed. Utterly vulnerable.

At the sight of him, unchecked fear like he'd never seen before engulfed her green eyes. His heart stopped cold.

"Dance?" Will asked quickly.

She gazed up at him as if he'd sprung a four-foot span of longhorns, and could he blame her? But all he knew was that he had about three more seconds before she'd bolt — maybe not literally, but he'd lose this chance forever.

"Read my lips, darlin'," he said. "Would you like to dance?"

Her gaze actually focused on his mouth as if she were translating every word. She blinked. "But there's no music playing," she said.

"If that's your only objection, it's easily remedied."

Will glanced toward the stage where the band stood, only then noticing he and Lacey had the attention of everyone in the room. He gave a short nod to the band's fiddle player, and with a swift eight-count they launched into a sprightly rendition of "Chattahoochee."

Will took Lacey's hand to lead her onto the dance floor. She remained rooted where she stood, although now with that familiar wariness. He considered it an improvement while still falling far short of dispelling his concern.

He tugged on her fingers. Lacey resisted. She *did* look like a rosebud in her flowered dress. And as irresistible.

He squeezed her hand reassuringly. "Though you've cordially invited me to," he teased, "I *won't* bite you — Cinderella."

That brought a bit of the old green fire to her eyes. "Yes, but *I* might," she returned, "because I'm *not* Cinderella!"

131

He laughed. "That's good. 'Cause, darlin', I'm no Prince Charming."

And, knowing he could resist no longer, Will pulled her into the security of his arms.

Lacey hadn't danced the Texas two-step in over eight years.

"Relax," Will said against her hair as she stumbled through the first cadence. He could obviously tell. "It's like ridin' a bike, you know."

And it was. On her back, his hand, large and warm, guided her. His other cupped her fingers in his palm. He held her securely but with a respectful distance between them which seemed just right. It wasn't long before she lost herself in the enjoyable — and particularly thrilling — sensation of being squired around a dance floor by a rugged cowboy.

Step, step, slide. Step, step, slide. Now a two-handed twirl here, now eight bars of strolling there, and back again, facing each other. The steps felt as familiar as an old pair of boots, the rhythm as comforting as the gentle rocking of a hammock.

Lacey glanced up at Will with a shy smile. He grinned back, which drew her gaze once again to that fascinating mouth of his. Her own went dry as cotton as she jerked her

132

eyes straight ahead.

She didn't need this! Not now. Not yet.

"Thanks for asking me to dance, Will," she said politely.

"Well, you looked like you could use a little help there with Matt."

She pulled back enough to look him squarely in the eye. "I was in *no* need of rescuing!"

He shrugged. "Whatever you say. But Matt certainly needed a hand, because it was lookin' aces to apples he was about to get punched by somebody, the only question being whether by Lee, myself — or you."

Lacey laughed, surprised that her indignation disappeared. "You're right. I guess I owe you my thanks, too, for keeping me from making a spectacle of myself."

"Oh, I wasn't savin' you from that. I firmly believe that it sometimes takes nothing less than a public scene to get your point across."

"As you do at every opportunity?" she asked, wide-eyed.

He looked at her keenly. "I'm not one to dally around a matter, that's true. Leaves others too much wiggle room for interpreting the facts."

He glided her through a quick sequence

of steps. "Anyway, it just seemed to me whatever button Matt had pushed with you was sure enough a hot one." Will peered into her face. "You gonna tell me what was goin' on a few minutes ago?"

Lacey stiffened. Her sense of calm disappeared just like that, and she felt her guard go up like the slamming shut of an iron drawbridge.

Will's silver eyes turned as steely, but then he seemed to catch himself. "It wouldn't have happened to've been that power issue you told me about?" he asked. "You know, of havin' your choices cut off, taking away control over your life?"

Her defenses dropped as she stared up at him in astonishment. "How did you know?"

He didn't answer for a few moments, as if he were weighing his words. Then he said, "I *don't* know, of course."

He glanced away briefly, his expression bemused, before he brought his still meditative gaze back to hers. "Maybe it's only after a man comes out of himself a bit that he's able to see answers to some of the questions in his life he was unaware of before." His lashes flickered as he perused her upturned face. "Answers that were practically under his nose all the time."

Lacey wrenched her gaze from his, her

better instincts at war with her impulses. She wasn't exactly sure what had changed or why, but this man definitely wasn't the Will Proffitt she'd been keeping a healthy distance from for weeks now. Except, of course, for those few times when it seemed he'd understood, to a certain extent. And it was such times — like now — that made her more wary than ever.

The gentle squeeze of his thumb and forefinger on her chin drew her eyes back to his. "Won't you tell me what's on your mind, Lacey?"

She became aware that the band had segued straight from Alan Jackson into Shania Twain's "Any Man of Mine," which the girl singer in the band wasn't half-bad at, injecting the words with the same sassy, take-all-of-me-or-nothing-at-all tone as the original.

So maybe it was that, or his encouraging tone, or the genuine interest in his eyes — or maybe it was her overwhelming need to be understood — but Lacey couldn't resist Will any longer.

She gave a small sigh. "Oh, it's simply perverse, the whole situation. It started with Matt turning me down for financing at the bank which, even though I was told my projection of income wasn't good enough, I suspected there was something else going on. And sure enough, Matt as good as admitted just now that he'd axed the loan to guarantee I'd need a big strong cowboy to rescue me — with him in the starring role! And if that weren't enough, city hall denied my application for a business permit, too!"

Her throat got tight again just thinking about it. "I can't believe it, Will, I really can't. It literally astounds me, although I don't expect you to appreciate how much. I mean, this is just how business gets done around here, and if I'm going to live in this town, I better get used to it, right?"

"Not necessarily, Lacey," Will said. He was back to his old forbidding self, and looked not the least happy with her estimation of the code he lived and breathed. Well, that was just too bad! He'd asked her to tell him what she was upset about — so fine, she'd laid out the facts as she saw them, and if he couldn't handle it, that was his problem!

"If you don't mind my asking," he said curtly, "why did you need a loan in the first place?"

Lacey hesitated, then figured she might as well come out with it and let him do his worst. It wasn't as if the situation could get any more discouraging.

"I needed financing for the resource center I'm starting for the girls in Abysmal. To give them . . . choices."

She waited, wondering if he'd drawl one of those cutting comments that virtually slayed her. At the very least he'd cock a sarcastic eyebrow at her which spoke volumes — and none of them good.

But Will's face was dead serious as he said solemnly, "You mean you'd be doin' the kind of thing you've wanted to, working with people to help them help themselves?"

Lacey stopped in her tracks, so the couple behind them narrowly avoided plowing into Will. He got them both back into the flow with a few smooth moves she barely noticed, she was still so surprised — and, she discovered, excited.

"Yes," she said. "Yes, exactly. That's what Lee's been doing at my house in the afternoon, working with Daddy and me to turn the house into meeting rooms.

"He told me what happened after I left those years ago. You've got to believe I had no idea what he'd been put through." She looked askance at Will. "You did a very thorough job of getting people to keep the secret. I've been meaning to thank you for that — for Lee's sake."

He didn't say anything, but she knew by

the tightening around his mouth and the almost imperceptible nod he gave her that he got her message that he had been out of line coming down on Lee. She supposed it was the best she would get from him.

"So, how did you come up with the idea for a resource center?" he asked.

"Actually, it came to me one day when I was talking to Jenna Barlow about her future here in Abysmal. She was about ready to light for Houston, where her cousin is — or even farther away — and I couldn't help thinking she'd get there and be completely out of her depth and become dependent upon who-knows-who. It just seemed she has so much going for her — so much fire and spirit — I hated to think of her losing one bit of it because she'd made a bad choice, thinking that the only way to make somethin' of herself was to get out of Abysmal and go looking for her happiness by way of a man taking care of her. And all I could think was, I can't let that happen. Not again . . ."

Lacey couldn't believe it when her voice grew thick with tears. She cleared her throat but it didn't help. Tucking her chin to hide her reaction from Will, she blinked rapidly and decided to go on. Needed to go on.

"I also wanted to do something that

138

was . . . fulfilling to me. And this center for girls really does that, if you can understand."

She didn't dare look at him, afraid she'd once again revealed too much of herself to this man when she'd have been best to keep her emotional cards closer to her chest — and her heart.

Then Will said quietly, his breath ruffling the hair at her temple, "I'd like to."

He'd been so stoic as her story had tumbled out of her, continuing to glide her about the dance floor, which was having the effect, she noticed for the first time, of drawing a lot of attention to the two of them. She found it did do her a world of good to catch a glimpse of Matt Boyle, looking rather poleaxed, on their way past him.

Behind him, Lee gave her a broad wink.

Of course, they *were* dancing pretty close. Sometime during the last song, Will had pulled her nearer to him.

And it had happened so . . . naturally.

Well, she *had* been pouring her heart out to him. She could still barely believe that she would to this man, even while she hadn't been able to stop herself. She needed to do it. For whatever reason, it seemed to her Will heard her and validated her purpose as no one else had yet, not even her father or Lee — and they were the ones supporting her most with their help.

But she hadn't told them much as to why, and with Will . . . telling Will about her reasons for starting the center, even if the real reason was far from being revealed — simply felt unerringly true. And it was one of her goals to listen to and heed such moments.

Lacey lifted her chin, found Will regarding her intently, his face only a few inches from hers, and quickly located her own gaze elsewhere in a continuation of the other dance they'd been doing all evening.

"Tell me more," he murmured into her ear.

Those three little words sent an even more potent surge of electricity through her, making her stutter. "W-well, um, I — I actually got the idea to start a resource center when I was trying to come up with a way for Mother and Daddy to stay in their house."

"Really? Is there a question of whether they will?" he asked somewhat urgently.

Lacey nodded. "The house is paid for, but the maintenance, taxes and insurance on it are pretty steep, as you can imagine."

"How have they maintained it up to now?"

She hesitated, then remembered: heed the moment. "Nicolai. It was part of the agreement when he built the house for Mother and Daddy that he pay for its upkeep each month. But he isn't doing that any longer."

"You're kidding." Will swore under his breath. "What kind of a man leaves his wife's kin in such straits?"

"But I'm not his wife. Not anymore."

"Sure, but it's still his responsibility to keep the house up, especially if he promised to."

"Oh, that wasn't the issue. Nicolai was perfectly willing to continue paying for the house."

He looked completely confounded. "Then why . . . ?"

"I refused to take anything from him, Will." She lifted her chin. "So now you know. It was my choice. I'm the one who's put my family into this position."

His expression was a study in speculation, his eyebrows practically touching in the middle and the lines of his rough-hewn face set even more severely than usual.

Lacey made herself shrug as if she didn't care. "I know it's difficult for you to believe, for anyone to believe, but it's true. I did give up the fairy tale. And I'd do it again in a heartbeat."

She bit back her next words, but then decided to let them fly. Because she *didn't* care anymore. It was too much to keep

141

inside. "The problem is, no one else wants to let go of the fairy tale. Matt Boyle and Dale Willis are just two of the people in town who are trying to keep me up on a pedestal."

Too late, she realized that once again her voice had risen, and if every eye in the place hadn't been glued to the two of them before, they certainly were now.

She didn't care! It was high time everyone gave up the image of her as a sweet little fairytale princess!

"What on earth will it take for people to get it through their heads that I'm *not* some damsel in distress waiting for Dudley Do-Right or Prince Charming or any other man to come riding up on a white steed and save me?" she demanded.

Will didn't bat a lash at her exasperation, even though it was aimed directly at him. Instead, he answered mildly, "Maybe because you haven't put a fine enough point on it."

"Meaning?"

"What do you say we give Matt Boyle — and a few other people — a load of the real McCoy?"

She shook her head. "How?"

"Just keep followin' my lead, darlin'," he said with a mysterious air.

He danced them over to the stage. The fiddle player stooped and Will said something into his ear. The man gave a nod, signaled his boys to stop the music, and started up in the next moment with the familiar strains of Brooks & Dunn's "I Am That Man."

And Will led her to the center of the dance floor again.

It was impossible for her not to give herself up to the moment. Her body felt like the music itself, lilting and fluid, each movement like the notes, one lingering into the next, building upon each other.

And all the while the words of the song floated about them, words of promises made and meant to be kept, of staying true to the end, with never a hesitation, never a doubt. Of giving all in complete surrender, for that was what it took to truly love a woman.

She was vaguely aware that they had the floor to themselves, was achingly aware of the man who held her, who seemed tuned to her every movement or thought. Or wish.

All too soon, the song wound to an end, but Will obviously wasn't going to let the moment dwindle away without the Proffitt embellishment.

"Think we've given people enough to convince them I've stopped believing you're a princess on a pedestal and they can all follow suit — or should we take another spin around the dance floor?"

She clutched his shoulders with both hands, trying to keep her balance, trying to keep her sanity.

"I told you before, Will, I'm not looking to get rescued," she protested, but her voice was reedy and faint.

"That's because you haven't been even the least tempted with anything you'd need rescuing from," he murmured as his mouth covered hers.

Lacey's breath suspended as every nerve ending in her body focused on his kiss.

Through a haze of pure feeling, it occurred to Lacey that had she felt one tenth of this kind of warmth from Nicolai, she would never have left him. She'd have stayed forever, would have been helpless to turn away from it. Or him, no matter what he had done. . . .

Panic enveloped her then, and with a choked cry, Lacey wrenched her mouth from Will's as she pushed away from him with all her might.

Everyone was staring at them. Everyone. She didn't care. She pressed her palms to her cheeks. They were burning. Her pulse pounded in her ears, her breath coming in

gulps. Will's breathing seemed pretty uneven, too, his chest rising and falling almost
in perfect unison with hers. His gray eyes
were dark and umbrous, like a full eclipse,
frightening and fascinating at once.

He slowly lifted one hand and ran the
edge of his thumb across that lush lower lip
of his, still glistening with their kiss.

That's when she knew: if there was any
rescuing needing done, it was for someone
to save her — from herself.

She didn't know what to do. She couldn't
go back into his arms; she'd lose herself if
she did. Lacey knew that as surely as she
knew her name. But impossibly, not to face
what she felt there seemed as completely
wrong for her, too.

No, she didn't know what to do. So she
did the one thing she could think of, that
had worked before. The choice that was still
open to her.

Lacey turned and walked away.

CHAPTER SEVEN

Lacey stormed out of the bank and hit the sidewalk on Main Street, angry strides taking her to her father's pickup. She was aware of passing by without greeting more than one townsperson who bid her good morning, aware that the fact would be all over Abysmal by noon of how she'd been on a royal tear. Speculation as to why would run the gamut from a hangnail to a hundred-year feud; severity would be gauged from a minor hissy fit to a boiling-over pot of bearcat stew.

Well, she didn't care what they thought! She was through with being manipulated, maneuvered, controlled, steered or otherwise tricked out of having a say as to what happened to her in this town!

Most of all, though, she was angry with herself. She couldn't believe she'd let down her guard with that man again!

Because it hurt. It hurt a *lot*, even if she

knew that was her problem and not Will Proffitt's. She should have known better than to confide in him a few nights ago at the town social, to trust him with even a little bit of her heart.

Except in the few moments he'd held her in his arms, she had felt understood and supported by him as she never had by any man, most of all Nicolai.

Her step slowed. Then she remembered, too, how out of control and completely vulnerable she'd felt. And Will had taken advantage of her! Her pace picked up with renewed vigor.

Lacey reached the pickup and yanked open the door, determined to keep up her head of steam all the way out to the Double R, when just down the street at the tack and feed, she spied the cattle baron himself loading bags of something into the bed of his truck.

She couldn't help but deem it a golden opportunity. She marched toward him, her fury building with every step.

Will looked up and saw her coming, and a smile touched his lips until he got a gander at her militant stride. And her face.

"This is *it,* Will Proffitt!" Lacey said, stopping a foot in front of him. "You've gone too far this time! Way too far!"

Slowly, he pulled his leather gloves off, looking for all the world as if he were getting ready to head inside for a leisurely glass of iced tea. "You mind tellin' me what you're talking about?"

"I wasn't quite sure getting back at Matt or proving something to the town had been the entire story the other night, and today my hunch proved out." She stepped toe to toe with him. "You're deliberately making it look like we're involved, first at the dance and now by making things happen for me down at city hall and the bank!"

She pointed a finger at his chest. "I don't know what game this is you're playing and I don't care! I just want to know what it's going to take to stop the almighty Texas Cattle King from manipulating other people — and me! — once and for all. Because the last thing I want is for people to think you and I are a couple!"

He moved her finger to one side as if it were the barrel of a gun. "A couple of what?"

"Don't be obtuse! You know what I mean. Like it's hands off of me for any other man in town!"

"I thought that was what you wanted," Will said mildly. "No bothersome frogs hoppin' around your feet and tryin' their hardest to kiss the princess."

"That," Lacey said through clenched teeth, "was low."

They locked eyes in a tussle of wills that clocked in at a good thirty seconds, during which Lacey saw not one bit of the man who'd listened to her with such empathy, who'd provided her with such comfort by simple virtue of hearing out her concerns.

The disappointment was crushing.

She was shocked when tears filled her eyes, profoundly aware she had let her emotions get the better of her — again! — and with the worst person she could do so. But how was she to be any different? How was she to say what she needed to say, be who she needed to be, even feel what she needed to feel — *wanted* to feel in order to be alive — without letting down her guard and making herself so . . . so vulnerable?

She whirled away from Will, hoping with all her heart he hadn't seen the glistening in her eyes, but he caught her arm, spinning her back around.

"Lacey, wait —"

"Let me go!" She tried to pull away but it was futile. He took her other arm and drew her close enough they were practically nose to nose.

"No, I won't let you go," he said in a low,

angry voice. "You got somethin' to say to me, I want to hear it, all right? And if you've got a problem with me, fine, I want to know what it is. I can handle that, too."

Stunned for the second time in less than a minute, she stared up at him. "Really?"

"Really." He shook his head imperceptibly. "But not here."

She didn't need eyes in the back of her head to know the doorway to every store and shop up and down the street had a head stuck out of it like prairie dogs peeking out of their holes.

"Where, then?" she asked.

"Let's step inside to Lee's office. He's gone to Amarillo to do some buying for the store."

She nodded, and in the next few seconds he'd guided her into the tack and feed, past an openmouthed Jimmy Ray, to the back of the building.

Lee's office was modest but tidy, and it even had a worn leather sofa up against one wall. Will took Lacey there and sat her down. He remained standing himself, slapping his gloves against his thigh as he gazed down at her, gray eyes brooding.

"All right," he said. "I'll own up to the fact that yes, I was trying to give people the impression we were an item."

150

"But why, Will?"

He cut her one of his self-reproaching glances. "Let's just say it seemed preferable to people thinking you and Lee were one."

That brought her up off the couch. "I swear, Will Proffitt, when are you going to let go of that? I am *not* interested in Lee!"

He marked her stance and tone, and nodded briefly. "I'm glad to hear it," he drawled. "As for engineerin' a situation to get your stuff approved with Matt and Dale, I didn't talk either of 'em into anything they shouldn't have done in the first place."

"What do you mean?"

"I mean after our conversation the other evening, I looked into the matter, and the situation was almost exactly what you'd said. Although on Dale's part, I give him credit for good intentions. He was only thinkin' to protect you —"

"But I don't want anyone's protection!" she interrupted. "I am *not* a princess waiting for Prince Charming, and you know it!"

She felt herself getting all choked up again, but she wasn't going to turn away this time. "I thought you understood that about me, Will," she said, her gaze imploring.

He reached out as if to touch her, then seemed to think better of the gesture and dropped his hand to his side. "And I believe I do. But you know convincin' everyone else in town isn't so easy as changing the name on your mailbox and puttin' on your old blue jeans. We've already had this discussion, Lacey."

"Then what *is* it going to take for everyone to just let me be me?"

Will ran his fingers back through his hair. "Well, I had thought going to Dale and Matt and taking 'em to task was going to help. I've got to say in Dale's defense that if he acted protective, it was because the picture of you he has in his mind is not as a countess but as this bitty tow-haired girl who used to come in with her daddy to pay the water bill when he was town clerk. I mean, he hasn't had much chance to know you as an adult woman who's got her own ideas and opinions. After all, you left town when you were nineteen. People haven't gotten the opportunity to get acquainted with you personally — and for all your talk of wantin' to be one of the gang, you haven't let 'em."

Lacey sank her teeth into her lower lip in thought. It made sense. She hadn't had much direct contact with Dale after she'd outgrown tagging along with her father. In fact, no one, really, had seen her develop into herself, from an unseasoned girl to a grown woman.

As for not letting anyone in town get to know her now, yes, she had to admit she'd been keeping people at a distance. It had simply been a gut reaction, especially since she was getting into some pretty deep emotional territory with her reasons for starting her center — reasons, at this point, which no one knew.

"I guess I can understand Dale's reaction," she admitted. She shot Will a questioning glance. "But what about Matt?"

Will shifted on his feet, looking abruptly uncomfortable. "Yeah, Matt . . . well, Matt was thinkin' he was some kind of Wall Street shark in training or somethin', which I'll own is partially my fault. So it seemed to me it was my responsibility to personally set him straight and make it right for you."

Lacey frowned. "You're responsible for Matt's behavior? How?"

"A month or so ago I asked Matt to sit on another loan," Will answered, and she saw the tips of his ears turn red. "I've since made that matter right, but I knew at the time he'd gotten it into his head this was the way things were handled once you got of a certain standing in town."

His gaze was direct. "But things *aren't*

handled that way, Lacey. At least not by me. I may not always conduct my business in the manner people'd like, but I'm not just looking out for my own interests and concerns, and who cares about the consequences to others. Just like you're set on not being seen as a princess, I am *not* some all-powerful cattle baron with a dozen puppets on strings that I yank on just for the pleasure of seeing 'em jump. And you'd know *that* about me, if you'll just take the time to think on it."

Lacey paused to think back to how he'd treated her that day by the barn on the Double R — with concern for her health and respect for her pride. How he'd behaved the day they'd built the chute out in the pasture — with interest in her perspective and sensitivity toward her beliefs. And how he'd responded to her frustration just now, with forbearance and consideration — even when under attack from her.

At the realization, Lacey sank back down on the couch. She looked at Will ruefully. "You're right. I owe you an apology, Will. All I can say in explanation is that I must be reacting to having lived for eight years with someone whose every thought and action was to manipulate me and keep me under his thumb."

"You mentioned that once before," Will said in a quiet voice. He left off the idle movement with his gloves. "About being vulnerable and having it used against you as a weakness."

No, she wasn't sure she wanted to open this emotional can of worms, especially with this man, but it struck Lacey that the matter was festering in her, affecting what she did and thought. And she remembered how she had vowed she would not let that happen to her. Couldn't let it happen to her. She'd die inside.

She drew in a deep breath, for courage.

"Yes, when it comes to exploiting someone's weaknesses, Nicolai is . . . the best." Lacey concentrated on her laced fingers as they rested on her knees. "Or maybe I should say he *was* the best. The best at manipulating me so I barely knew I was being maneuvered. Everything he did or said was calculated out to the nth power. Trying to argue a point with him was a lost cause. He had a way of picking apart my reasoning, coming at me again and again, questioning every point, until I became lost in the logic and had to admit defeat."

"Is that how you ended up back here?" Will asked, his voice as hushed as hers.

"No. I stayed — that was my surrender. I

gave in, gave up, thinking that was how marriage was. How it had to be. H-how the rest of my life would be." She clamped her lip between her teeth, a bid for precious control.

After a moment, she found a measure of it, and went on. "I'm ashamed to admit I stayed in that existence for a long time. I abdicated my wants, my needs, my opinions to Nicolai's, I wanted so much for my marriage to work. But some sense of what was right for me survived inside me, and eventually I sort of developed a different way of dealing with him, one that preserved as much of myself as I could. So instead of trying to fight a battle I couldn't win, or giving in completely, I withdrew emotionally, protecting myself. Still . . . compliant, but not conquered."

Lacey made herself raise her eyes to Will's. "That's when the battle started in earnest."

He went very, very still. "Did he hurt you?"

"No. Nicolai never raised a hand, not even his voice, to me. Not once."

She saw him digest her statement, his expression a meditation in reflection, and Lacey wondered if her worst fear had just come true, where she revealed the emotional abuse she'd endured — and not have had it understood how devastating it had been to her.

If he didn't, she didn't think she would be able to stand it. The vise around her throat was almost to a strangling point, making her feel she had to fight for every breath.

Then Will said, "It sounds like a living hell."

The choke hold eased, just enough, for Lacey to swallow the sudden lump that rose to her throat. "It was," she said, "although I'm not sure most people would see it that way. I mean, there are women who deal with far worse situations than I ever did every day, women who truly are fighting for their lives. And I . . . I was living out a fairy tale every girl dreamed of living with my very own handsome prince. In people's eyes, I'd have had to have been crazy not to be happy. B-but I couldn't be, no matter what people said, no matter what he told me —"

Lacey stopped, dropping her chin again, as the memories temporarily overwhelmed her, filling her chest to bursting.

Out of the corner of her eye, she saw Will sit on the sofa a few feet away from her. He leaned forward, elbows on his knees, not looking directly at her, either.

"What happened to make you see you couldn't stay, Lacey?" he prompted gently.

She held up one hand, needing time, so that she could make herself breathe deeply, reorient herself. She was no longer in Nicolai's grip. She was here: home, in Abysmal. And Will was by her side.

"Nicolai saw he was losing his influence over me," she said after a moment. "I'd learned to never let my guard down, never relax, never let my emotions show. Never show weakness. So he tried to get control over me through other means — through other people. That's what that big mansion for my parents was about. He knew I'd put up with a lot to make them happy. But that tactic only worked on me for a while. Finally I knew that no matter what would happen to me or my parents, I couldn't stay. I had to leave Nicolai Laslo if I was going to survive. And that's how I ended up back here."

She didn't have the nerve to look at Will but kept her chin tucked and her gaze fastened on her clasped hands. Then his large one covered them, warm and reassuring.

"So that's why it's so important to you to start this center for girls, isn't it?" he said softly.

His understanding was like a salve on her soul. "Yes. But no one knows that. No one but you."

Silence pervaded the next few minutes as, eyes squeezed shut, Lacey struggled to master her emotions. Will grasped her fingers in his, linked and laced them together in silent support, which instead of calming her made her even more upset.

A tear escaped her lids and fell, then another and another.

And suddenly she was in his arms, his broad, hard chest beneath her cheek as Lacey cried as she never had in her life.

But she supposed that was how it went when one was healing a heart, so when you at last found an understanding ear to listen to what you had endured and validate your experience, only then could you get to the bottom of your fears, start to feel the feelings you needed to that would help you to mend — and go on.

"I'm sorry, Will," she said, sniffling and making a weak attempt to push out of his embrace and pull herself together which he rejected with the steeling of his arms around her.

"No, I'm sorry, Lacey," Will murmured into her hair. "Sorry for what you went through. That wasn't right, what he did."

He lifted her chin so she had to look at him. Through a blur of tears, she saw his smoky gaze travel over her features with an expression of contrition. "And I'm sorry if I've done anything to remind you of him. I hate to think I have, even though I know I can be a control freak who has a difficult time letting go of bein' Iron Will Proffitt long enough to recognize what people need instead of me thinkin' I know what's best for them."

"A control freak?" Lacey was surprised into asking.

He slanted her a droll glance. "Lee's assessment of me, not mine."

A bubble of laughter rose in her, surprising her even more. "Oh, I don't know about that. You've been pretty responsive and considerate of my needs," she admitted shyly.

The penetrating look he gave her was drawn out for several seconds before he said huskily, "Well, don't go pinning a medal on me just yet. It's occurred to me I *haven't* been all that aboveboard in my actions lately, and the experience has sure enough shown me I could do with some improvin'. Man," he gave an impatient click of his tongue, "maybe I *am* a — how did you put it? — an interfering, domineering ring-tailed control freak, I believe was *your* expert appraisal."

Now it was Lacey's turn to blush with shame. "I was pretty condemning, wasn't I?"

"Darlin', if you could bottle the blisterin' quality of your tongue, you could sell it for varnish remover and make yourself a cool million."

They both broke out in laughter at that.

"You're miles from being like Nicolai, Will," Lacey averred. "I mean, he was controlling for the sake of power alone." She paused, thinking, her fingers idly tracing a pattern on his shirtfront. "Maybe your way of having to run the show is more a sign that at heart you care deeply for the welfare of people, you know?"

Will said nothing in response, just brushed a lingering tear from her cheek with his thumb, his palm cupping her cheek.

At that tender touch, Lacey found herself held motionless as she'd been before, torn between flight and fascination, at war with her instincts and her experience. For the scene which leapt vividly to mind was as he'd danced with her, every move attuned to hers — before he kissed her.

As then, Will now evoked in her the same fear. It was the last she must face, the biggest and deepest of all.

And what Lacey feared most was that she

could never trust or love a man again, because both made you vulnerable, and she'd learned from Nicolai Laslo the infinite number of ways such vulnerability could be used against you. As much as she believed in her strength of spirit which had seen her through her eight-year ordeal, she feared as greatly that the damage done to her heart during that time was irreparable.

She stared up at Will, their faces so close she could see every nuance of gray in the irises of his eyes. So often had she perceived them as shadow, she was startled to discover how clear and sharp, like shards of glass and slivers of silver, was each striation. Clear and sharp and steady.

Could she trust Will? But even as the question rose to her mind, she knew this wasn't a matter for intellectualizing or rationalizing. It was a matter of the heart, of feelings and instincts which came from a place inside a person that wasn't logical, though that didn't make their influence any less powerful.

Her gaze dropped to his mouth. His lips parted on an intake of breath, and she watched, completely captivated, as he came closer. . . .

She felt as if she were balanced high up on the ridgepole of a house, with the prospect of a devastating fall on either side of her. And she knew in a flash of comprehension that only if she maintained her equilibrium, held on to her perspective and stayed true, kept her chin up and kept aiming for the stars, would the risk be worth it when she finally spread her wings and took off.

Lacey wrenched herself from his arms, pushing herself to her feet, where she stood shaking like a leaf.

Now was not that moment. Not yet.

"Lacey . . ." From behind her, he touched her hand. On pure reflex, she jerked away, knowing she must seem as erratic as a weather vane in a storm.

"Th-thanks for everything, Will," she babbled.

She meant for lending her his ear and shoulder to cry on — it had meant so much to her for him to give them to her — but Will obviously chose to take another meaning, because he said from behind her, "If you need anything for your resource center, Lacey — I mean, more than someone to run interference with the bank or city hall — you've just to say the word, you know that, don't you? I mean, now that I know what it's all about, I'd like to . . . to lend a hand."

Lacey turned to look at him, and she

couldn't prevent a tinge of sadness from creeping into her voice as she said, "I didn't tell you what had happened at the bank and city hall — or with Nicolai — so you could take care of things for me, Will."

His eyebrows lowered and his mouth tightened but he didn't say anything in reply.

Which was a good thing, Lacey reflected as she walked out. She wanted to hold on to the real support he had given her which she'd need in the coming weeks to take care of things herself.

The headlines said it all.

"Laslo: Countess Needs Help" shouted the *Dallas Morning News* spread out on the kitchen table. "Fractured Fairy Tale? Not So, Reveals Count" screamed the *Austin American-Statesman.* "This Time, Prince Charming Waits For Cinderella" was the header blazoned across the *Houston Chronicle*'s entertainment page.

"Entertainment!" Lacey exploded. "I can't believe it! Not only is Nicolai feeding the media this crazy story about us, he's turned our personal tragedy into entertainment!"

"He sounds awfully sincere," Rachel said reasonably, pointing to one article.

Leaning over the table, Lacey shoved the papers together into a pile as if hauling in poker winnings. "Of course he does! He's a master at this sort of thing, twisting and turning the facts to his advantage, portraying the situation in a way that seems completely logical and so of course everyone believes it's true!"

Her mother made an impatient sound. "But he's saying he'll take you back. How is that twisting the facts?"

Her arms still outstretched around the heap of newspapers, Lacey bent her head briefly. "Can't you see, Mother? He doesn't want *me.* He wants control over me."

Rising, she stalked to the kitchen wastebasket, depressed the pedal to open the lid, and threw the newspapers into it, letting the lid slam closed again with a satisfying *clack.* The gesture accomplished little, though, in relieving the claustrophobia-like fright that threatened to engulf her.

It didn't help that they'd had to close every curtain and shade in the house to protect themselves from the prying eyes of the dozen photographers and reporters who'd camped outside since the news hit the street earlier this morning.

It wasn't that the story was big news, Lacey knew, it was just terribly juicy. And Nicolai would have known it would take something scandalous to draw this kind of attention to her.

Fighting panic, Lacey crossed her arms over her middle and clutched her sides, but it didn't stop her shaking. She should have seen this attack on her coming, or at least something of this sort. But she hadn't, which made her fear she wouldn't be able to anticipate where and how he would strike next. That her own responding actions, or lack thereof, would affect his tactics almost pushed her over the edge into sheer hysteria.

Drawing a deep breath, she tried to go over the facts, one by one, as she knew them.

From what she could tell, Nicolai had apparently given an interview to a French newspaper in which he had "reluctantly revealed for the first time" how he was devastated by their divorce. A newspaper in the States had picked up the story and interviewed Nicolai themselves. That's when he'd strategically spilled his guts. The problem was, he didn't just reveal their private and personal business, he out-and-out lied about how one day they had been happy and so in love, and the next she'd bewilderingly announced she didn't want to be married any longer. As if she changed her mind and direction as capriciously as a feather floating on the breeze!

According to the rest of the story, which had by then been picked up by a number of major newspapers around the country, Nicolai had tried to convince her to stay and seek counseling, but she'd not only refused, she'd up and left one day without a goodbye, walking out with just the clothes on her back — making her sound even more erratic.

Unbelievably, it got worse. More than merely painting Lacey as a rather emotionally unstable woman, Nicolai had no trouble convincing the interviewer that she was, in his loving opinion, "deeply psychologically troubled," since it was obvious no woman in her right mind would not just leave him, refusing all monetary support, but also return to the wretched existence he'd plucked her from. And the coup de grâce? He said it had nearly destroyed him to learn she was scrabbling — unsuccessfully — to make ends meet and keep her parents in their home, when he would give her the moon without her asking!

Lacey pressed her knuckles to her lips, combatting tears of utter terror. She'd gathered he would know where she'd gone, but how would he know even a little about what she was doing here in Abysmal? It made her feel personally violated, defenseless within the one domain where she thought she could count on a measure of privacy and protection.

How did he know what she was doing, since any outsider would have stuck out like a flamingo in a crowd of crows? Who here would have told him?

And most importantly, did he know about her resource center? For some reason, she felt it would be the most grievous invasion of her privacy of all.

At least, Lacey comforted herself, Nicolai wouldn't actually invade her sanctuary. He'd cut off his right arm before he'd step foot in Abysmal.

She didn't even know her mother had come up behind her until Rachel said, "What did Nicolai *do* to you, Lacey? And this time I'm not going to take an evasion for an answer! Did he drink? Cheat on you? Strike you . . . or w-worse?" She sucked in a fortifying breath. "I want to know the truth!"

Lacey turned and looked at her. Yes, why not tell Rachel the truth? What did she — or actually, either of them — have to lose?

"Yes, Mother," Lacey said in a flat voice. "Nicolai Laslo is guilty of all of the above. Every day he hit me — with a barrage of criticism on everything from my looks to my speech to my background. Every day he betrayed me — betrayed my trust and love, making a mockery of them by wielding them over me to impose his will on me. Every day he abused not some substance but *me* — used me to keep from dealing with his own lack of self-worth by sucking away at mine."

Her expression dazed, Rachel walked jerkily to the table and sat down. She shook her head. "But Nicolai knew when he married you what you were and where you'd come from."

Lacey took a chair kitty-corner to her mother's. "Yes, he knew — I was a nobody. Someone he could feel superior to in every way. And someone he could assure himself he'd always have power over by taking a poor little sow's ear and making a silk purse out of her. But things didn't go his way from the first."

"So why . . . why did you stay?" Rachel asked.

"Because, at first, I was in love with him," she answered truthfully. "He was my husband, and I was committed to him and the marriage. And even after things began to change between us, it was nothing overt, nothing you could define as a real reason to leave, like physical abuse, infidelity, addiction. You couldn't even call it verbal abuse. Nicolai was always ever so cordial in his suggestions for me and how I should behave. But the message behind those helpful words . . . the message was toxic. He meant to make me believe I could do nothing, and was nothing without him."

It registered in Lacey's mind that her voice had evened out, as if her mother were the one needing a calming hand. "What he did was just as wrong as if he'd hit me or cheated on me, I've come to realize. It was a form of emotional abuse. And Nicolai was a master at it. It took me a long time to realize the number he was doing on me, but I finally did. So I took steps to . . . to protect myself, still thinking to stay in the marriage if not be happy. But —"

She hesitated, then decided there'd be no use holding this back, either. "Nicolai sensed I was slipping from his control. That's what building the house was all about. Leverage — over me, through you. And I'm almost ashamed to admit it worked for a while, kept me from leaving Nicolai long after I should have."

Rachel gazed at her, and Lacey noticed how weary her mother looked, even more worn out than she'd seemed when Lacey had first come back and Rachel had been dealing with that development. And now there was this to contend with.

Still, she said with conviction, setting her hand over Lacey's, "I — I'm glad you told me, honey."

Lacey swallowed, trying to rid herself of the lump of emotion which sprang to her throat so frequently these days. "I'm glad I did, too."

And she was. Not that she felt particularly unburdened, only that now the explanation was done. Hopefully, it brought her one step closer to putting the marriage behind her.

She heard a key in the lock and the front door open. A cacophony of voices assailed her ears.

"Mr. McCoy, how's your daughter? Has she seemed unbalanced?"

"When's Cinderella going back to the count?"

"You're just a carpenter, sir. How do you expect to keep up paying for this mansion without Laslo's support?"

Her father's voice was a low murmur, so she couldn't make out what he said in reply, but it likely wasn't anything too informative, judging from the closed expression on his face as he came into the kitchen.

She rose and went to give him a fierce hug. "Oh, Daddy, I'm so sorry for bringing this trouble on you and Mother —"

"Now, none of that," Hank said, giving her a squeeze and dropping a kiss on her forehead. "I've dealt with infestations of termites that were more trouble than that pack out there."

"Were you able to find Jenna Barlow and let her know not to try to come to work here today?" Lacey asked.

"I sure enough did."

Rachel glanced at the clock over the kitchen sink. "What are you doing home so soon, though? I thought you were determined to finish up that job over at the Canfields'."

"I was, till I got drift of what was takin' place in town." Hank looked at his daughter with sympathetic eyes. "The whole of Abysmal is abuzz with your news, darlin'. Since you came back, people've been wonderin' what had happened, and they're kinda perturbed they've had to learn it from the outside."

Lacey stiffened. "And?"

He scraped his palm down his cheek. "I have to tell you, Lacey, this isn't gonna die down like you were hopin'. Those media people have been pumpin' everyone in town for information. So far they haven't said a word, but that's mostly because they don't know what's going on. Pretty soon, though, they're liable to start telling as much as they do know about what you've done since you came back."

She pulled out of her father's embrace. "They will, will they? Well, they can tell the media what I've been telling them all morning — it's none of their business!"

Just then the phone rang for what was surely the fiftieth time that day. Her mother rose to go into the den and listen to the message after the answering machine picked up, in case it was someone they actually wanted to talk to and not another reporter.

A moment later, Rachel returned. "Lacey, it's Lee."

Lacey crossed the floor to pick up the extension on the wall. "Lee?"

"I'm out front in my pickup callin' on my cell phone, Lacey. Didn't think you'd answer my knock on your door with all those vultures hoverin' there."

"You figured right."

"How're you doin'?"

Lacey grasped the receiver in both hands. "Oh, Lee! I so didn't want for something like this to happen. I truly hoped by leaving Nicolai and asking for nothing that —"

The line crackled with static. "Uh, look, Lacey, these kinds of calls can be listened in on so I don't want to stay on the line. You want me to come in?"

"I'd really like that." The noise level outside rose, she suspected because of Lee's presence. "I guess the only way to do this is for you to just muscle your way through the paparazzi to the front door and I'll have Daddy let you in. I'm afraid they're going to get in your face again," she apologized, remembering how he'd told her of the media's assault on his privacy eight years ago. "Are you sure you want to go through that?"

"Depends. Do I get a crack at any of 'em along the way?" Lee asked.

Lacey actually laughed. The restricting collar around her throat, which in the past six hours had become so tight she hadn't been able to choke down a bite of lunch, eased just enough. "Well, try to keep it legal, okay?"

As she hung up the phone, Hank was already on his way to the door. A few minutes later he appeared with Lee. He looked grim.

"Man, if I wasn't crazy already, bein' held hostage in my own house by a buncha low-lifes like that would sure enough make me that way," he said.

Lacey bit her lower lip to keep it from

trembling. Lee caught sight of the movement and was immediately contrite. "I'm sorry, Lacey, I didn't mean that."

She nodded jerkily and decided she'd need to get a grip on her emotions.

"The worst of it is, we may be in for a real siege," she explained. "So I guess the best thing to do is figure out a strategy, just as if we were defending ourselves from one."

Rachel fetched the iced tea as they all sat down at the table.

"First," Lacey said, "I think the best way to head Nicolai off is to give him no ammunition. I mean absolutely nothing. If people in town feel they have to start giving comments, fine. I'm not too happy about that, but anything anyone else says is minor to getting the scoop from one of us, you know?"

"But, Lacey —" Lee began.

"I know it's a lot to ask," she said to him, her father, too, "but I'm going to have to count on you two to run the gauntlet outside for Mother and me when it comes to getting supplies and such. I don't want to give the media even a chance at me. And I don't want to put Mother through that sort of experience."

She turned to Rachel. "I'm sorry, Mother. It's going to mean you'll be confined here with me for who knows how long. But I really think the media will get tired of getting nothing from me pretty quickly and go off in search of more exciting prey."

"But that's what I was just going to say," Lee said uneasily. "I don't think your keepin' mum is necessarily going to make the story die."

Lacey shook her head. "Why wouldn't it?"

"Well, the reason I came over was because I'd gotten word of how Laslo is now tellin' everyone that he's prepared to come to Abysmal and win you back on bended knee."

CHAPTER EIGHT

Lacey's glass hit the table with a crash, breaking it and spilling tea all over the tablecloth and lone newspaper which hadn't made it into the trash. The amber liquid spread quickly, darkening the newsprint as if to seal her fate.

"Honey, you're bleeding!" Rachel cried.

Hank grabbed Lacey's wrist and pulled her over to the sink, where he stuck her hand under running cold water before pressing a clean towel to it.

After a moment he drew back the edge to reveal a jagged cut on her index finger. She stared at it with detached interest, as if she were looking at someone else's hand.

Hank examined the wound. "Doesn't look like you'll need stitches although it wouldn't hurt to take you on down to Dr. Wolf and have him confirm that."

That jolted Lacey out of her detachment.

"No!" She jerked her hand out of her

father's grasp. "I'm not going out there! I won't! I can't!"

She whirled away from his puzzled gaze, and her mother's frightened and Lee's apologetic ones, clutching her injured hand, towel wrapped around it, to her middle.

"*Why* would he come here?" she cried, bending over her swaddled hand, cradling it like a baby. "I just want to be left alone."

Her father's fingers gripped her upper arms from behind. "Now, now, Lacey, it'll be all right. I promise it will."

Oh, how badly she wanted to believe him! Wanted to be the little girl who could trust with all her heart again. Could she? Just for a while?

"You don't know how Nicolai thinks," she whispered.

"I tell you what," Hank continued. "Let's see if we can get a hold of Nicolai and sit down and talk things over. I'm sure if we jest tell him you're done with him and there's no goin' back, he'll see he's got to give this fool notion up."

Drawing herself up with a deep breath, she turned around. "It wouldn't work, Daddy. Nothing will work. You don't know Nicolai. But he knows me. He made a science of studying me and my reactions, like I was a bug in a jar! He lives to manipulate me just this way, putting me on the spot and making me dance to his tune whether I want to or not!"

"That's what you can do," Lee spoke up. "You can tell the media your side of what happened. Tell 'em how Laslo treated you." He gave a short nod. "After all, this is the good ol' U.S. of A., and you're America's Cinderella. The public's sympathy'll go straight to you."

Sadly, Lacey looked from Lee to Hank. They were such good men — good and honest and straightforward and sincere. She didn't want to have to tell them, too, try to make them understand the kind of unscrupulous and downright diabolic motivations Nicolai operated under. Why, they must still be inconceivable even to her, for why else would she not have anticipated that he wouldn't let her go so easily?

And even knowing the lengths he had gone to to control her during their marriage, she had a feeling, with this new ploy, that until now she'd seen only the tip of the iceberg.

That desperation gripped her again, worse than ever before. She couldn't escape it, couldn't escape him.

Lacey looked beseechingly at her mother, the last person in the room who might understand her predicament, if only by virtue of having knowledge of her daughter's anguish. "Mother, you know what Nicolai is like, what he did to me. I told you, it's all about gaining power over me. Surely you can see how impossible it would be to have anything to do with him."

A war of uncertainty clashed in Rachel's eyes. Then she burst out, "Oh, Lacey, I'm so sorry! I didn't know what he'd done! How could I? I was only thinking of you, especially when Nicolai said he'd do any-thing for a second chance with you —"

Lacey went cold as ice. "He said that? Where? When?"

"He called a few weeks ago!" Rachel confessed, clearly beside herself. "I didn't tell him about your center, only that you were working very hard to keep us in this house! I wouldn't do you that way, honey, you've got to believe me. I just couldn't stand seein' you unhappy and I didn't want to see you walk away from what might be a real nice life, if it could be saved at all."

Lacey dropped her chin, shoulders slump-ing, her heart heavier than it had been in months. She *knew* she was right about Nicolai's motives, knew she wasn't being overly suspicious or unduly unfair. She knew it to the bottom of her feet and the tips of her fingers. And honestly, she wasn't asking for someone to bail her out, solve her problems for her. She wasn't even asking for advice. She just wanted someone to understand! Just one person, and somehow she knew it would make all the difference in the world to her.

Just one single person, she hoped, that's all. Just one —

"Lacey!"

Her head shot up. Someone was pounding on the front door so hard it creaked on its hinges.

"Lacey, open up! It's Will!"

She flew to the door and flung it open, heedless of the crowd waiting for just such an event. But Will, with the strategic jab of an elbow here and the shove of a sturdy shoulder there, kept the reporters from getting even a foot inside.

He lunged across the threshold and slammed the door shut behind him.

"I just heard," he said, breathing hard. "I would have been here sooner but I've been out on the northeast section since before dawn trying to save a mama cow and her calf that'd gotten through a fence and were stuck in a wash."

She gaped at him. A bead of perspiration trickled down one temple, his hat was askew on his head and his shirt was torn at the shoulder seam. He was dusty and dirty, smelled of horse and cow, and the rowels on his spurs were gouging divots in the thick oriental carpet underfoot, but she didn't care! It took every bit of her willpower not to throw her arms around him and kiss him.

His gaze took in hers and grew dusky and intense. Then it fell to her hand, still wrapped in a towel.

"Lacey, are you all right?" Without asking, he reached for her arm and unwrapped it. He examined her finger grimly. "Where's a first-aid kit?"

"Th-there's one in my bathroom," she replied. "Upstairs."

Will swept her past the rather surprised-looking threesome at the foot of the stairs and took her down the hall to the bathroom off the bedroom she had moved into when she'd come home. He sat her down and quickly found the first-aid kit in the gilded French provincial armoire standing against the far wall.

He washed his hands clean in the sink, then knelt on one knee in front of her, the kit at her side. He took a leisurely glance around the room as he unrolled a length of gauze, his gaze finally coming to rest on the pink velvet chaise longue she sat on.

"If I didn't know better I'd think I was in Las Vegas," he observed.

Lacey had to smile. "It's rather overdone, isn't it?"

He held her hand in his as he daubed antibiotic cream on her cut with a swab. "To say the least. How'd this happen?"

"I broke my tea glass."

He raised his eyebrows in question.

"Lee had just come in with the news that Nicolai had told the press he was prepared to come to Abysmal to g-get me."

Lacey ducked her head, batting her eyes to keep sudden tears from falling. She heard Will muttering above her.

"Why's he doin' this, Lacey?"

"As if he needs a reason!" she said bitterly. She pushed her hair back on a sigh. "I've got to think, though, that his popularity abroad has gone down since the divorce. Prince Charming sort of loses his charm without Cinderella at his side. And so far as his popularity in the States, it always seemed to me that while he was the real nobility, it was my pauper-to-princess story that people related to."

She lifted her chin and tried a weak smile. "Sort of an Americanized version of Kate Middleton. Except I wasn't the daughter of wealthy parents. I was the everyday, average

183

girl next door, and that made it even more fascinating, I think."

Lacey watched him bind the cut snugly but not too tight, then secure the gauze with tape. "So now it seems I'm in for a battle royale of some kind, because I'm not giving in. I can't. And I know Nicolai enough to know he won't give up."

She rubbed her forehead wearily. "I'd so hoped to avoid such an ugly, very public scene. But it seems unavoidable at this point."

"I know your divorce wasn't exactly time capsule material, but I'm surprised you escaped the media's scrutiny as long as you did," Will commented. He scrutinized his handiwork, then dropped the roll of tape and scissors back into the kit and closed the lid.

"I know. I think that's mainly due to the divorce being so quiet. There were no affairs to expose, and no nasty custody battles or settlements. And because I came here, to Abysmal."

She concentrated on smoothing down a wrinkle in the white tape on her finger. "I've wondered if maybe, too, leaving him was the one action Nicolai hadn't banked on my taking, and it's taken him this long to work all the angles out again. I don't think it occurred to him that I wouldn't want at least one thing from him he could leverage against me."

"Then it seems the man has a blind side," Will said. "And that means he can be defended against. The question is how."

"I'm afraid, though, it's going to take more of a countermove than just sitting tight." Lacey looked at him. "My parents think I should meet with Nicolai, Daddy for me to tell Nicolai there's no chance of a reconciliation, and Mother for me to hear him out in case there is. I c-can't do either of those, Will. They don't understand that to give an inch where Nicolai is concerned would be emotional suicide. He's a master at twisting and turning around every little thing you say. There's no way to win."

He brushed her hair back, his palm coming to rest against her cheek. "Then don't say one word to Laslo."

She couldn't prevent herself from leaning into his caress. "And Lee thinks I should tell the media everything Nicolai has done, just spill my guts and let the press run with it. Try to style myself as some kind of heroine! I can't do that, either. Put the entire history of my personal torment and pain out there for everyone to see?" Even now, the thought brought back every bit of her terror. "I can't."

"Of course you can't," Will told her quietly.

"But I have to do something!" She gripped his wrists as he took her face between both hands and gazed at him in appeal. "I have to, or he'll come here to Abysmal. I don't think I could stand that, Will, if he did, and found out about my center for girls. He'd destroy it, I know he would, because he'd know it was the one thing I couldn't stand to have destroyed."

"He won't get that chance —"

"This is *my* town, my corner of the world. My safe place. He can't come here, do you understand?"

His hands were large and warm on her face as he shook her gently. "I *understand,* Lacey. And don't worry, he won't."

He hadn't given her a way to keep that from happening, but somehow she believed him. Believed they'd come up with some plan.

Will chewed on the corner of his mouth for a moment. "So you're not sure what to do to keep Laslo from getting a toehold in your life again. Then let's go over what you *won't* do — like sit down and talk with him, or tell your side to the world."

That seemed like a good approach. "I

don't want to fight him, either. I refuse to sink to his level. I wouldn't be able to live with myself if I did. And I truly don't want my parents or Lee or people in town to be harried into hiding out in their own homes, but the media is not going to go away empty-handed, especially as long as there's the prospect of Nicolai arriving."

Will scraped the edge of his index finger across his chin. "Let me get this straight. What I'm hearin' is that the press won't leave without a story — but it doesn't have to be the real story. And Laslo's going to come to Abysmal in hopes of makin' a scene that'll flush you out into the open — unless he's given a pretty good reason not to. So —" he cocked one purely devilish eyebrow "— why not top him by makin' a scene of your own? A scene to end all scenes. *And* one that keeps your real private business out of the news for good."

"Like what?" Lacey asked warily.

"Well, Laslo's not going to rest till he's got you back as his countess, right?"

"Yes —"

"And he's going to try every trick in the book to wangle you into makin' such a commitment, isn't he?"

"Yes, but —"

"Yes, but *everything* hinges on you bein'

187

available at this point. I mean, a man can stomp and threaten all he likes, but the fact is he can't bid on a comely young heifer if she's already been sold, you know what I mean?"

Lacey blinked as comprehension hit her. "You aren't suggesting . . ."

He grinned wickedly. "Oh, but I am. And since it seems I'm already in the proper position . . ."

Still on bended knee, Will grasped her fingers in his and whipped off his hat, pressing it to his chest like some cowboy come a-courting. "Lacey McCoy, will you do me the great and glorious honor of becoming my bride?"

"You can't be serious!" She tried to tug her hand from his, but he was having nothing of it. "Really, Will, we can't get married just to force Nicolai to abandon his game."

"No, that's true." He looked charmingly disappointed. "But we can get engaged. That'll work just as well, I should think. 'Sides, you got a better idea?"

Lacey frowned. "Not at the moment, certainly, but you must realize it'll be a long time before this all dies down in the media. Months, at the very least, during which we'll have to keep up a pretty extensive charade."

He shrugged. "I'm game if you are."

"And what happens afterward? I mean, we can't stay engaged forever. People'll start to wonder. Sooner or later we'd have to, you know, d-do something —"

"*Do* something?" he asked innocently. "Like what?"

Her face heated up like an oven turned on full blast. "Honestly, Will, the whole idea is insane!"

"Is it?" He set his hat on his head and took her other hand in his, squeezing them reassuringly. "I don't see any other options, and you don't have much more time. Why not just go with this plan for now and hope some better idea occurs to you when you're not under the gun? You'll think of something, and when you do then we'll just announce we're callin' off the engagement. Sound fair?"

He was right there. She didn't think she'd be able to come up with anything better, and she was running out of time before Nicolai would make his next move. Still . . .

She gazed at him solemnly. "I told you before, Will Proffitt, I don't need someone to rescue me."

"Then don't consider it rescuin'. Think of it as . . . as my returning a favor you did for me."

"*I* did you a favor?" Lacey asked in amazement.

"Sure you did. A couple of 'em. In gettin' to know you, you've spurred me into takin' a look at myself and takin' care of some old business that's been hanging around for years now. Business with Lee." His lashes flickered and faltered slightly. "And with myself."

"Such as?" she prompted softly, on tenterhooks at the prospect of at last getting a glimpse inside Will Proffitt.

"Oh, I'm not for tellin' you just right this minute," he said with one of those self-reproaching half smiles.

She nodded. For some reason at that moment, she was willing to trust that what she wanted to know, needed to know, would be revealed to her in its proper time.

"In that case," Lacey murmured, "thank you, Will, for helping me out. I appreciate it."

Gray eyes glowing like coals, his gaze roved over her features in a way that stole her breath away. "Not a'tall, Lacey. Not a'tall."

She didn't know how long she sat there in the thrall of his perusal until she found herself drawing in a shuddering breath.

"So," she said with a nervous glance

toward the doorway, "you're absolutely positive it's going to take a full-out, attention-stealing, cover-Grandma's-eyes scene to thwart Nicolai?"

"Like I already told you, darlin', my experience proves it takes nothin' less if you're serious about gettin' your point across. And the more you act like you've settled right back into the routine here, the better. Which means —" he trailed a fingertip down the bridge of her nose "— just be yourself, Lacey McCoy."

She smiled and kept on smiling as he pulled her to her feet and, linking her arm under his, escorted her to the top of the stairs. There they paused, looking at each other as if embarking upon a great adventure.

In a sense they were, she realized. An adventure in which, she discovered, it was very nice to have him at her side. And on her side.

"Let's go meet our public, Cinderella," Will said, and he ushered Lacey down the stairs to the whistled tune of "People Will Say We're in Love."

With an expert eye, Will surveyed the crowd which had collected on Main Street in the noonday sun. To his estimation — and satisfaction — it looked like the whole town had turned out. Even little old Mabel Atkinson, who never left her house except for church, was there, sitting in her wheelchair under the shade of an umbrella held by her great-granddaughter.

A low and steady murmur, like the buzz of bees on a summer afternoon, filled the hot, dry air. From his vantage standing in the bed of his pickup, he noticed that several of the media folk with cameras had sweated through their shirts. From the looks on their perspiring faces, he'd guess they were wondering how they'd ended up on assignment in this two-bit, backwater Texas town.

Which meant they were going to appreciate him giving them an excuse to pack up and hightail it back to the coast.

"Ladies and gentlemen," Will said in a loud voice, raising his hands to get people's attention. The noise died immediately, faces rapt. Will hid a smile.

"Now, folks, you're probably wonderin' why we called y'all together today," he said in his best Starbuck, with the whole of the town the gullible Lizzie. "And I know many of you are busy people with better things to do than stand out here in the sun and listen to me jaw-jackin'. So I won't beat around the bush."

He turned to the woman who stood next to him, the real person who'd brought these people out in droves. Even now, more than a few of the television cameras were rolling — and aimed straight at Lacey.

He was glad she'd had no chance to spruce up, because her jeans, boots and simple sleeveless blouse struck just the right chord of Texas casual. Except, with the way the sun reflected off her golden hair and her eyes bright as pale green gemstones, she still looked like she belonged on a throne instead of standing in the bed of a pickup. He could see her anxiety about this whole plan, and he remembered her horror of being exposed, of having everyone stare at her like an animal in the zoo. Still, the look in those eyes was trustful as she gazed back at him.

He wouldn't let her down. Why and how it had become so important to him that he come through for her, Will hadn't the luxury of pondering right now. All he knew was that her placing her faith in him gave him a feeling like no other he'd had in his entire life. And that he'd done or said something to earn that trust made him feel like a king — and somehow blunted the lingering echo in his heart of his ex-wife's parting words.

Taking her hand in his, Will gave Lacey an encouraging wink. "Go on, girl. Tell 'em your news."

She returned his wink with a grateful smile before turning toward the crowd.

"That's right, folks," she said with a lot more confidence than he knew she felt inside. "I'm not going to keep you in suspense any longer. Frankly, I'm about to burst with the news —" she paused dramatically and he had to admire her, for the throng held its collective breath "— because Will Proffitt has asked for my hand in marriage, and I've accepted!"

There was a three-count of dead silence. Then the whole street erupted.

"I'll be dogged!" Old Man Wilkins exclaimed.

Vernal Adams clapped her hands. "I knew it! I just knew it. Didn't I tell you there was sparks a-flying 'tween them two?"

Lacey's mother looked stunned. Her father wore a frown.

"Miss McCoy, over here!" came the shouts from the news people. "Miss McCoy! What about the count?"

They clambered over each other, jockeying to get their mikes into closer range of her. Will was glad he'd had the foresight to place Lacey and himself out of their reach. He snugged her up against his side as one man struggled to hoist himself into the bed of the pickup, camera and all.

Will set his boot on top of the man's knuckles and smiled benignly. "Just so's you know, we Texans are kinda particular about our trucks, and people layin' a hand on one are like to find themselves missing a few digits, if you know what I mean."

The man seemed ready to protest until he squinted up — and up — at Will. "Uh, sorry. Didn't mean to offend."

Will lifted his boot. "An honest mistake, I'm sure."

Lacey's parents had found their way to the front of the crowd, and Will released her so she could bend down to give them both a hug. Just then Lee had reached the other side of truck and motioned him close. Will stooped.

"What d'ya think you're doin'?" Lee asked furiously. "I swear, Will, if you're usin' Lacey to get back at Matt Boyle again — or me — I'll hog-tie you to a mesquite and leave you out on the range for the buzzards to make a meal of you, and don't think I won't!"

"I'm not usin' Lacey," Will said in a low, angry voice. "I'm helpin' her out of a jam and that's all!"

"Oh, really?" Lee's eyes widened. "Then you're makin' a pretty big idiot of yourself

195

in the process!"

Getting called an idiot didn't set too well with Will, considering how Lacey had once said how if a man was going to make one of himself over her, he'd do it without her help.

"Actually I was savin' *yours,*" he returned. "This kind of grandstanding is right up your alley, and there *you'd* go lookin' the fool again in front of the whole town. At least I have the wherewithal not to lose my head and let things get out of hand."

"Yeah? Well, I guarantee an idea this foolhardy would never've crossed my mind, Big Brother." Lee wagged his head back and forth in wonder. "Nope, I'd have to say this is all your doin', and don't kid yourself it's not. All's I want is a front seat at this sideshow, 'cause I'm real interested in seeing how you're gonna get yourself out of this one."

"If it does the job and gets Laslo off Lacey's back, that's all I care about," Will said tersely.

"That right?" His brother cocked his head to one side. "Well, sounds to me like you might have a few people to convince besides the count."

Will straightened. Sure enough, the initial shock of his announcement had worn off and people were beginning to try to make

196

sense of it.

"Lookie there!" somebody said, pointing at Lee and Will, obviously picking up on the angry undertones in their conversation. "I *knew* Lee was still sweet on Lacey."

"D'ya not got eyes in yer head, ya durned dummy?" came a censuring voice. "Didn't you see her with Will at the Summer Fling? He kissed her right in front of everybody!"

"Yeah, but then they had that set-to down in front of the tack and feed," piped up another, "and I *know* I heard Lacey say somethin' about them not bein' an item!"

"That's right! And what about that mornin' she and Will got into a ruckus in her Daddy's truck right here on Main? Weren't nothin' loving in that discussion."

Will looked at Lacey. Her expression of disappointment made the bottom drop out of his stomach.

"This isn't going to work, is it, Will?" she said softly.

"Now, why do you say that?" he demanded, wondering for just a split second if Lee was right. *Was* he a prize fool who was going to make an idiot of himself in front of everyone — again — by not knowing what a woman really needed from him?

No! He wouldn't let Lacey down!

"They don't believe us," she answered.

197

"They can tell — even Mother and Daddy looked at me strange."

"Tell what, for crying out loud?" The hurt in her eyes at his tone about killed him. He reached out, chafing her upper arms with his hands. "What can people tell, Lacey?" he asked more gently.

"That we're not . . . not in love." Her chin dropped, and she looked as forlorn as a motherless calf. And nearly as forsaken. "Th-thank you for trying, though, to help me. It means a lot to me that you would."

He wasn't giving up that easy. Will set his teeth into his upper lip, thinking hard. After a moment he said, "So we're not in love. Is there nothing we could do to persuade people we're the real McCoy?"

Her head shot up. "What do you mean?"

Drawing her a little closer, he swayed back and forth, a harkening back to when they danced. "I'm just wondering if we might come up with a convincing . . . demonstration."

Lacey's eyes flared in understanding. Then her gaze dropped, almost unwillingly, to his mouth.

He'd seen that happen before, more than once. In and of itself, it was about as powerful a glance a woman could give a man — one that stirred *him,* at least — and as much

198

of a clue as to her secret desires as he would ever get.

It was all the encouragement he needed.

"Will you trust me, Lacey?" Will asked with a slow smile.

"Wh-what?" she said dazedly, gaze still glued to his mouth.

"Will you trust me?" He enunciated the words.

She nodded jerkily.

He took her hand and turned back toward the crowd. "Like she told you folks, I've asked Lacey to marry me and she's accepted. But we've failed to seal the engagement as yet. And y'all know Iron Will Proffitt." Several people gasped at his use of his nickname. "When it comes to closing a deal, I don't like leaving any detail undone."

With that, Will pulled Lacey into his arms. He had the briefest glimpse of the surprised O of her mouth before he covered it with his.

CHAPTER NINE

Like the last time, kissing Lacey was as close to a dream as Will could get standing up. She had the moistest, softest lips. Will gave himself over to the purely luxurious feeling of kissing the boots off of Lacey McCoy.

She didn't seem to be holding back much, either.

Slowly, as if coming to him from across a misty pasture at dawn, he became aware of shouts and whistles and applause getting louder and louder until they replaced the pounding of his heart in his ears.

Will drew his head back, shaking it slightly. "I think we convinced 'em," he said hoarsely.

Arms still wrapped around his neck, Lacey opened her eyes as if waking from a hundred-year sleep and looking just as thoroughly kissable. "Wh-what?"

He couldn't resist planting one more kiss on Lacy's delicate nose. "I said I think we've got everyone here believin' we're in love. And since every one of those cameras is still glued to us, I'll wager the rest of the free world'll believe it, too, after those videotapes hit the air waves."

"Yes, but . . . but will Nicolai believe it?" Lacey asked, uncertainty touching her eyes.

Will trailed a finger down her cheek. "It doesn't matter if he does or not as long as people are on our side. He'll have no choice but to accept it as gospel or risk looking like he's standing in the way of true love, and that's never a popular position for a Prince Charming, ex or otherwise."

She appeared to think the logic of this over for a few moments before she broke into a heartened smile. "You're right."

She hugged him, quite spontaneously, right there in front of everyone, and that feeling filled him all over again, near to bursting, as the roar of approval swelled once more.

Then over her head, Will noticed Lacey's parents. Both of them wore an expression of worry.

And behind them stood Lee, still shaking his head in wonder as if he'd never stop.

Proof of their success came late that evening in the form of an announcement on the radio in which Nicolai Laslo, via a clipped, formal statement issued by his "people," said indeed he would not presume to encroach upon another man's claim to his ex-wife, the countess, and that his greatest wish was that Mr. Proffitt, despite exhibiting the rather crude behavior his occupation seemed to require of him, might appreciate the jewel he had found and treat her accordingly.

"How dare he!" Lacey charged. "After the way he treated me, he's got some nerve insinuating you're some . . . some . . ."

"Almighty cattle baron?" Will asked. "Or maybe Texas Cattle King?"

Lacey opened her mouth to protest, then realized he had only parroted back her own invectives of him. Instead she gave him a quelling glance, at which he grinned. She'd grinned back before becoming struck with an unaccountable attack of shyness that had her blushing and dropping her gaze like a schoolgirl.

They sat under the stars by the pool, Will with his bootheels propped up on the edge of a stone planter. Rachel had just popped out the back door to alert them to the announcement by switching the news program they'd been listening to to the outside audio speakers.

Before returning inside, her mother had glanced at her questioningly and, riddled with guilt, Lacey had been unable to hold her gaze. It had to seem to both her parents that she'd jumped straight from the frying pan into the fire.

On the ride back to the house after their own announcement, she and Will had discussed keeping the ruse their secret for now. Lacey wasn't happy about misleading her parents, but Nicolai had already gotten to her mother once. Even though Lacey had impressed upon her mother the importance of speaking not one single word to Nicolai if he had the audacity to call again, she also knew how her ex-husband could manipulate others into telling him what he wanted to know without them having the slightest clue they'd spilled the beans.

And Lacey was under no illusion that they'd heard the last of Nicolai Laslo.

So she and Will had to make this engagement look like the real thing. And apparently, they had put on a pretty convincing show. That's how they were able to sit in privacy out on the patio. The media had departed — and the rest of the town evidently decided the two lovebirds could use the time alone.

Alone — with Will Proffitt.

Lacey sneaked a covert look at him, his head tilted back and profile illuminated in the rippling light reflecting up from the pool.

He had been so purposeful and confident and dependable today — or actually, so she was learning, as always. He'd said he felt he had some improving and perhaps some proving to do, and as far as she was concerned he'd succeeded. Lacey was endeared beyond measure by his support and understanding. But she couldn't quite trust those feelings. Didn't trust *herself* to.

And if she wanted to know why, it was in his kiss. When Will pulled her close and fit that rich, wild mouth against hers, she was scared to death. For she recognized it as a longing to completely let go in a backward free fall into pure romance.

Of course, she'd had a hearty sample of that sensation today, standing in that pickup bed, and she'd survived it all right. But there she'd been safe, of a fashion. Both times Will had kissed her, they'd had the constraints of being out in public to keep a rein on themselves, and they had both known it. Maybe that's why he'd kissed her only under such conditions.

And maybe that was why she had a mortal fear of what would happen should he ever get her alone. She didn't know if she'd be able to hold back — and letting go completely was not an option.

Because it *would* mean giving herself to him completely, emotionally. And Lacey couldn't do that, give herself to a man that way again.

"You're awful, awful quiet over there for someone who just pulled off the biggest victory since Teddy Roosevelt charged San Juan Hill," Will said.

"I feel more like Davy Crockett holed up in the Alamo," she returned absently, slouched in her chair. "Holding off the enemy for now but on a doomed mission anyway."

"Oh, come on now. That doesn't sound like the do or die Lacey McCoy I've come to know."

"It doesn't, does it?" she said tartly, then sighed. "I'm sorry, Will. It's just that this business with Nicolai couldn't have come at a worse time."

He sat up. "How's that?"

She pushed herself up straight in her chair, too. "Oh, I've been finding out how difficult it is to secure money for the girls' center. We've gotten our nonprofit status, and while I think I can count on the people and businesses in the area to understand the benefit of such services and give what they can to the effort, I'm having a hard time convincing people at the county and state level of the center's advantage."

"Do you need outside support that much?"

"Yes and no," Lacey said. She drew her knees up to her chest and hugged them, wondering if she wanted to get into this subject with Will. She'd told no one about this part of her undertaking.

Will leaned forward, elbows on his knees, his interest obvious. The breeze, normally stiff and heated, was lazy and cooling tonight. It felt like heaven.

"You see," she said slowly, gaze fixed on the shimmery depths of the pool, "I don't regard this center as being just for girls in Abysmal and the surrounding area. My hopes for what I can do may be a little ambitious, but I really believe the need for opportunities for girls to build self-esteem and to realize their potential isn't confined to rural areas. I may be wrong, but I think programs like mine aren't needed just in small towns, but bigger towns and small cities, and even big cities, the biggest of all. I met a lot of people when I was a countess, and they were girls and young women in *all* situations, poor and rich, talented and average, minorities and majorities."

She spread her arms. "And meeting them, what I saw was that they wanted the life they believed I had. I'm not saying that young girls should stop dreaming about falling in love and wanting the fairy-tale ending it brings, because that's what being young is about. But to see love as rescuing them from life's trials isn't realistic, not when real love is about endurance and trust and working together to make that love the best it can be."

Lacey rubbed her forehead pensively, wondering if she should go on, but needing to, more for herself than anything else. Because she'd seen Jenna Barlow's face this afternoon as she'd gazed up at the two of them, arms wrapped around each other's waists in a pose of seeming devotedness. In Jenna's eyes, Lacey had seen confusion — and disappointment.

She'd been feeling disappointed in herself ever since — for letting herself fall into being rescued again.

"What's really bothering me is that getting this center here up and running isn't going to be enough. I want so much to show these girls that before they go looking for love, they need to learn how special they are. Because it's only after they've realized they deserve the respect and best effort of everyone around them, and that they shouldn't accept one bit less, that they'll find the real love waiting for them, the h-happily-ever-after kind, where they can just b-be accepted for being themselves —"

To her confusion, her voice broke on her last words, and for a moment Lacey struggled to compose herself, wondering madly what was wrong with her this evening, and if she had again made the mistake of revealing too much. Trusting too much.

She dared a look over at Will. His face was partly in shadow, setting his features into relief and more than ever making them appear carved in stone, and she realized suddenly she'd been going on as if lecturing him, for he had gone very, very still.

"So it's as simple as that?" he said in a strange voice. "That what girls — and women, for that matter — really need is as simple as acceptin' them and respectin' their feelings and choices, and having the people in their lives give their best effort to them?"

"I can't speak for everyone, of course," Lacey said slowly, "but I think . . . yes. I know that's what I need."

He actually looked as if he struggled to

control himself. Was it to keep from coming out with one of his terse comments meant to jerk her back to reality? Somehow she didn't think she could take that right now, and she set her jaw against the inevitable impact, against the fear . . . before saying, "Well that, I definitely can do."

And he reached across to take her hand to draw her onto his lap and into his warm, strong arms.

The closeness was exhilarating and death-defyingly frightening at once, like balancing on a high wire. But she couldn't let go and free-fall. Not yet.

Maybe not ever.

For when he lifted her chin with one finger and bent his face close to hers, Lacey's head snapped back reflexively, as if from a slap in the face.

Will dropped his hand and sat back slowly. Too slowly, as if he'd taken a blow himself. Well, her reaction had been extreme, considering that just a few hours ago they hadn't been able to let go of each other!

"Is there a problem?" he asked.

"Y-you don't have to k-kiss me," she stammered. She flashed a glance at his face, then quickly away again. How was it he could get her as agitated as a hen with a coyote in the coop in a matter of seconds! "I mean, there's no one looking."

"That's why I thought this'd be a prime time to give it a try," Will drawled. "Just the two of us, you know what I mean?"

His voice was pitched right between sexy growl and persuasive whisper. Lacey swayed toward him perilously before she caught herself at the last second. She set her palms on his chest. "And what I mean is we don't have to pretend right now. You know, that we . . . that it's more than . . ."

"More than a mighty case of the hots for each other?" he asked, blunt as always.

"Well, yes!" She blushed furiously. "Really, Will, just because we have this attraction, there's no reason to let ourselves call these emotions . . . more than they are."

She looked at him pleadingly, wanting him to understand this about her above all. "I — I can't do that, Will. Not again."

But it seemed on this subject he wasn't as sympathetic. In fact, his face turned to stone. "Of course. Better not to confuse this feeling for something more."

He released her, and she stood so quickly she almost lost her balance.

"If you don't mind my givin' you a little unsolicited advice —" he said.

"I have a feeling you'll give it even if I do mind," she interrupted, feeling more vulnerable than she had since that day beside the barn, and just as scared out of her wits.

He evinced no reaction but went on quietly and with conviction, "I can't deal you the aces, Lacey, until you let go of that hand you're holdin' on to. No one can."

Lacey stared at him. Was he right? Were her own fears stopping her and not the damage wrought by her marriage?

In her confusion, she lashed out.

"That's easy for you to say," Lacey retorted. "I bet you've never been at the mercy of another's power over you, even after they're no longer a part of your life! Or had the choices in your life taken away from you! I mean, look at what happened today! Suddenly I'm in this make-believe engagement to a man I'm not in love with, and he's telling me how to live my life!"

Will rose slowly, the stare of those wolflike eyes was as frightening as ever. "Pardon me, but *you* made the choice today to pretend we were engaged, and if you're not happy with that decision, you've got no one to blame but yourself."

Though her arms remained crossed defiantly, she was forced to consider his words. Yes, she had no one to blame but herself for being in this predicament. At the time, she'd believed she had been listening to her instincts, but who knew what had influenced her? Here she'd been so wary of not trusting Will, and now it seemed the real culprit was herself.

It struck at the heart of her, making her disoriented within her own head. She'd had a measure of faith in her instincts, but now she wasn't so sure what she was listening to.

Or perhaps she was listening, and what her intuition was telling her *was* to protect herself from this man.

When after a long moment she'd said nothing, Will muttered an oath and picked his hat up from the patio table, fitting it on his head with a rocking adjustment. "I get the picture, Cinderella. You can rest assured *this* Prince Charming'll know his part from now on."

Immobilized by her fear, she watched him go, wondering why this time following her instincts made her feel so desperately unhappy.

Lacey had to drag herself out of bed the next morning, which was definitely not like her. She'd tossed and turned half the night, and spent the other half in dreams about Nicolai, her parents, Jenna Barlow — and Will. In all her reveries, she'd been caught between trying to please everyone and trying to do what she needed to do to follow her heart. It had become a mantra she'd repeated over and over.

Still feeling cotton-headed and worn-out, she descended the stairs to the kitchen and poured herself a cup of coffee, hoping the jolt would revive her. Idly, she paged through the newspaper on the table and winced at the item headed "It's Out for the Count; Cinderella Opts for Lone Star Prince Charming."

Reading the article and seeing her name linked with Will's in print gave her a jolt like nothing caffeine could achieve. How could she have agreed to such a plan? she wondered for the hundredth time. Because the way it looked in hindsight was that she'd not solved her problems but rather compounded them, in spades.

To have her instincts so fail her terrified her.

"There you are!" her mother said brightly, coming into the room carrying a bouquet of fresh-cut roses from her garden. "I was out front talkin' to Ida Thornton, and she said to give you her best wishes on your engagement to Will."

"That was nice," Lacey said in monotone as Rachel, humming, filled a vase and began arranging the roses in it.

At least someone's happy this morning,
Lacey thought with yet another twinge at
her subterfuge. She hated misleading her
parents most of all.

"Ida wanted to know if you and Will had
set a date yet," she continued, bringing the
vase to the table and setting it in the center.

Lacey pressed her fingers to her eyes. "No,
we haven't set a date, Mother."

"Well, Ida was askin', I know, because the
church gets booked up earlier and earlier
these days."

She couldn't take it anymore. Lacey set
her forearms on the table, palms pressed
flat. "Mother, I need to tell you something."

Rachel glanced up from her fussing with
the flowers. "Yes?"

Her mother's face had lost that pinched
look she'd worn since Lacey returned to
Abysmal, she noticed, surprised. Rachel
looked cheerful and happy — and young —
for the first time in ages.

"Oh, nothing, I guess." Lacey dropped her
gaze. She couldn't tell her mother the
engagement was a sham, not yet. Somehow,
some way, she would think of how to tell
her in a way Rachel would understand —
and would make Lacey feel she hadn't sold
her soul to the devil.

As to whether it was to the devil she knew

214

or the one she didn't, she'd yet to figure out.

Then she spotted the yellow invoice lying on the table.

"Oh, did the computers finally come this morning?" Lacey asked, her own enthusiasm jump-starting at last. Except —

"Why is 'Refused' written at the bottom?" Lacey said. Her mother's signature was below it.

"It just seemed to me you wouldn't be needing that equipment right now, so I told the delivery man to take them back."

Lacey gaped. "You didn't! Mother, we need those computers as soon as possible. It's going to take weeks to get them set up with the right software, and we're already a week behind schedule!"

"Oh," her mother said in a puzzled voice. "But I was thinking now you'd finally be able to stop workin' so hard on this resource center."

Lacey couldn't believe her ears. "Of course, I'm going to continue working on getting the center up and running! Why on earth wouldn't I?"

Rachel met her eyes defiantly. "Well, for one you've been wearin' yourself to a frazzle over it! It's got you worried sick, and don't tell me it hasn't! And all I've been thinking about is that thankfully now you can relax, now that you're gettin' married."

Sinking back in her chair in bafflement, Lacey stared at her mother. For a moment she was at a complete loss. Then she became indignant, even as she realized she had no one to blame for this turn of events but herself. "Believe it or not, Mother, I'm not doing this just to keep myself occupied until some big strong man comes along to take care of me!"

"Don't you take that tone with me, Lacey Jane! I'm only trying to help!"

Lacey crushed the invoice in her fist. "What I'm saying is, even if I did marry Will Proffitt, I'd still be committed to this center."

Her mother looked at her sharply. "What do you mean *if*?"

Beyond overwhelmed, Lacey silently cursed her slip of the tongue. Obviously, her mother was no longer happy — and it was all her fault. Again.

"I . . . meant . . . when I marry him," she whispered the lie, despising herself for doing so. How had things gotten so out of hand, and so fast? Had she actually believed she could play Nicolai's game and come out ahead?

That old bromide about weaving webs to

deceive flitted briefly through her head before the doorbell rang, and rang again.

Why did she have the feeling that the news behind it wasn't good?

With a weariness that had nothing to do with lack of sleep, Lacey rose and went to answer the front door. Will stood on the stoop, looking grim as she'd ever seen him.

"I came to tell you as soon as I heard," he said.

Her first thought was that Nicolai had counterattacked. But no —

"Jenna Barlow's run away. Her cousin in Houston is getting married, and Jenna's gone to be her maid of honor. She left a note."

"And?" Lacey asked, expecting the worst. It came.

"She said she was going after her own fairy tale," Will answered. "Just like you."

CHAPTER TEN

Lacey spent the better part of the day in a whirlwind of talking to Jenna's father, the sheriff, and a few of Jenna's friends.

The story they pieced together was no fairy tale.

Jenna's cousin Carla had apparently been calling her, trying to entice her into coming down to Houston. As Jenna's friends told it, she'd refused, going on about how she had been helping the ex-countess Laslo get a girls' resource center up and running, and how she was going to learn about all sorts of things. Once she did, not just Houston but the world would be her oyster.

Carla had countered with how she was doing just fine without "broadening her horizons" — how else could she afford a new car? In fire-engine red, no less.

Still, Lacey learned, Jenna had stood firm — until Carla had dropped a bombshell: her boyfriend had given her a diamond engagement ring for her birthday. Yes, she — Carla Hayes — was getting married! It's what she and Jenna had dreamed of since they were little girls.

As fate would have it, Carla had told Jenna her news in a telephone conversation which had taken place the evening before the little drama with Nicolai had ensued. According to Jenna's friends, although she had kept the matter from Lacey up until then, wanting to handle it herself, this development had made her question why she was waiting to go seek her own happiness. Still, she had wanted to talk the matter over with Lacey. Unfortunately, Jenna had had no opportunity, since the very next morning Lacey and Will had announced their own engagement.

That evening, Jenna was gone.

The news devastated Lacey.

"She left because of me, Will," she said, her arms wrapped around herself as he ushered her into Lee's office at the tack and feed, the closest place around for her to find some privacy in which to come to grips with this calamity.

Even though the early evening sun filtering through the blinds warmed the room, she shook as if from a deep cold. All she could do was stand in the middle of the room, feeling impossibly hopeless and so very alone.

"Now, it's not your fault," Will said, coming up behind her. He didn't touch her, but Lacey moved away anyway, out of range of the energy which radiated from him like a force field. It was too close right now, too tempting to let herself become swept up in his presence again. She had to think. Think of what to do to bring Jenna back.

"But it is my fault!" she declared. "Jenna looked up to me as a role model, and what did I do in her eyes but jump from one marriage into another!"

She was struck afresh by her culpability in this matter.

"I'm going to get her, Will," she said definitely, turning toward him. "I've got to. She wouldn't have done this if not for me. I'm the only one who can convince her to come back, and I won't leave Houston without her!"

"Really?" Will drawled. "Now doesn't that sound just like me talkin'. I'm flattered, Lacey. I didn't know I held that much sway with you."

She recognized the old ploy of his. "Don't do me this way right now, Will, I'm warnin' you."

His eyebrows drew together. "All right, then. I'll lay it on you straight, even though you've had all kinds of objections to that approach, too."

Those gray eyes glinted. "The fact is, you can't make Jenna come back. She's eighteen, for starters."

"She's just a girl!"

"She's a young woman old enough to be on her own and makin' her way however she chooses. And goin' to Houston is what she chooses."

"No, it isn't!" Lacey cried, turning on him as if he were the cause of this mess. "She wants an escape from her problems! She wants to get out of Abysmal and away from her father!"

"You've just to say the word and I'll fetch her back here," Will said calmly. "Or fly you down to Houston to talk her into coming back — but only if that's what you want."

"Yes! No." Lacey shook her head in confusion, her hand to her throat, which ached with unshed tears. "I wanted so much more for her, that's all! That's why I'm starting this center for girls. Because of Jenna."

He took her by the upper arms, shaking her gently. "But it's not about what you want. It's her choice, Lacey. Hard as it is, you've got to let her make it herself."

"But don't you see, Will? There *is* no fairy tale. She's looking for something that exists only in her mind. And when she finds that out, I'm afraid the disappointment will destroy the best that's in her — her innocence and hope. A-and trust."

Will hesitated a moment, seeming to take in what she'd said. Then he took her by the shoulders and unceremoniously set her on the leather sofa like a little kid.

He sat down next to her and faced her squarely.

"All right, then. Let's take a look at the facts," Will said, businesslike. "Now, from what we heard today, Jenna was pretty dead set on pursuing some kind of fairy tale. You even told me once it was touch and go gettin' her to buy into what the center was about, and not just lookin' at it as a way of gettin' to bask in the glow of an ex-countess."

"I really did think I was making progress in that area, though," Lacey said. "And that's not just wishful thinking talking. I could get through to her every once in a while. She was a smart girl, a thoughtful girl."

"But still a teenager. So the way I see it is, you've given her somethin' to think about. Maybe that doesn't seem like much to go on, but it's got to have its effect as time goes by and reality sets in."

"That's what I mean, Will! I've *been* there, where Jenna is right now, thinking she'll find her Prince Charming like Carla did and never have to worry about another thing in her life. And when you find out how foolish you were to pin all your hopes on him . . . you feel you can't come back, because no one would understand."

"But *you* do," he said. He lifted her chin. "I'm not convinced it might not do Jenna more good to see what it's like out there in the world. All I'm sayin' is, don't think that the time you spent with Jenna is wasted, Lacey, or that there's nothin' that you can do from here to help her, if you'll just put your mind to it."

Lacey peered intently into his eyes, looking for any sign of insincerity or his humoring her. But she saw none, only a genuine believing.

She closed her eyes, thinking. What would have made a difference, not only eight years ago but all through those thousands of days she was gone — or even since she'd come back — that would have helped her to find the truth in herself to know what was right for her, and the strength to do it?

She opened her eyes and focused on Will. "I can let Jenna know she's loved, accepted and supported, and that I'm here for her no matter what."

She gripped his wrist, his hand still cupping her chin. "And that, if the world falls down around her shoulders, I'll be here to help her pick up the pieces and figure out how to go on."

His gaze ranged over her upturned face, the hardness she'd seen there a few moments ago now completely vanished, as if it had never been. "I think that'd help her a lot," he said softly.

A fullness suffused her chest, very different from the binding feeling she usually felt. This, she realized, was the good kind of tightness — as if she would burst from gladness.

Lacey squeezed Will's wrist, so strong and solid. "Thank you."

"For what?"

"For listening." She slanted him an embarrassed glance from under her lashes. "For *your* not trying to fix my problems."

In the golden light seeping through the slats of the blinds, she could see his lips lift into one of those irresistible smiles. "Am I hearing it correctly, or did you just tell Iron Will Proffitt he's not quite the domineering, interfering ring-tailed control freak who tricked you into getting engaged to him?"

Her face heated up like a Christmas bulb,

and she tried not to let that smile get to her. "I've always maintained that people can change. I certainly believe I have that capability. Why wouldn't others?"

"Why, indeed," Will murmured. "So — it looks like you've got a phone call to make."

He rose, and it seemed the most natural gesture in the world for her to take his hand when he offered it and allow him to pull her to her feet. He immediately dropped her hand, leaving her feeling bereft, although they remained standing so close she could feel his breath against her hair.

It felt very good to be with him this way, as it had when he'd provided comfort before. Very right. Every instinct in her shouted it to the rafters. She lifted her chin just as he dropped his, bringing their gazes into contact — and almost their mouths.

The moment suspended, then burgeoned and grew. Then as if choreographed since the beginning of time, she tilted her chin as he ducked his head — and their lips met in a stirring kiss.

The feel of him seemed as familiar to her as her name, yet new as the morning dew.

Perhaps that was because this kiss was not just his doing, but both their choice. For herself, she couldn't have even said why she made it, only that she had to. Had to feel emotional again. Had to let go.

Had to feel passionate again.

But the kiss was like an electric current that traveled through her body, making panic explode in her chest. "No! Will, I can't. I'm sorry. I thought . . . I could . . . but not yet!"

With a mighty shove born out of sheer terror, Lacey pushed Will away. She shrank against the arm of sofa, her heart pounding a mile a minute.

From the other side of the sofa, Will stared at her.

"I don't understand, Lacey," he said raggedly.

"That's right, you don't!" she lashed out, knowing she was being irrational but unable to stop herself. "You don't understand . . . what it was like. To be constantly on your guard because someone wanted to own you, heart, soul and body. But it wasn't about love! It was about domination, and he wouldn't be satisfied until he had complete power over me and at his mercy!"

She stopped to draw in a badly needed breath, and the hysterical shrillness of her voice resounded in her ears. She *was* hysterical.

Lacey covered her face with her hands.

"Do you think I want power over you,

Lacey?" Will asked, his own voice low but just as penetrating. "Do you think that's what this is about? I am not Nicolai Laslo!"

"No, I don't think that! But there is something that's keeping me from taking the risk of finding out!"

She tried to get a hold of her emotions, which were whirling with all kinds of impressions and sensations, not the least of which was a case of deep distrust of anyone or anything at this point. It made her question herself as to why she continued to feel this way. Was it truly because she'd lost all innocence and hope, that she could never completely trust another man?

She trusted her father, though. And Lee.

Forehead on her knees, she fought for calm, fought to get to the truth within her.

"I think," she said at last, "that having power and being in control are part of your makeup, though not all of it. I don't know what happened while I was away, but people must call you Iron Will Proffitt for a reason."

She raised her head and looked at him, waiting. Waiting for answers she had long needed.

His gaze searched hers, sounded its depths profoundly as if trying to find his own reasons to trust.

And apparently not finding any, for as the

seconds dragged on and on, the opportunity for them to both tear down barriers and reveal themselves to each other waned — and passed.

From opposite sides of the sofa, they stared at each other like two foes over a bargaining table, neither of which was willing to give an inch. But how could she give in, give more, until she got what she needed from him?

"It looks like neither one of us is willing to take the risk," Lacey said softly.

"It sure looks that way," he said, expressionless.

She felt inexpressibly sorry. Sorry for them both.

Will was as impassive as ever as he helped her to her feet, dropping his hand on her elbow once she'd gotten her balance. The drive home was equally silent, the goodbye terse.

The masks — both his and hers — as firmly in place as ever.

Lacey wiped down the last stretch of kitchen counter and rinsed the dishcloth before folding it and draping it over the faucet to dry. She let her gaze linger on the scene outside the window over the sink, where a glorious sunset was overtaking the western sky in true "big, bigger, just right" Texas style. Blazes of orange and red burst over the horizon with the subtlety of a Sherman tank, leaving bold tracks of vivid gold in the wisps of clouds.

She turned at the sound of footsteps coming into the kitchen.

"Finished with the supper dishes already?" Rachel asked.

"Yes. It doesn't take much to clean up when you've got an industrial-size dishwasher," Lacey observed. "It must take you a week to fill it when it's just you and Daddy here. I don't doubt you run out of dishes before then."

"Actually, I don't use the dishwasher much for just that reason," her mother said. "I'm kind of partial to hand-washing, anyway. Grew up that way and got used to it through most of my married life. I don't see much reason to change now. So you see, I wouldn't miss that dishwasher if I didn't have it."

Lacey nodded absently. She was still a little numb from today's happenings, first with the computers, then with Jenna's running away. Then with Will. She wanted to trust him, wanted him to trust her. And she did trust him . . . to a certain extent. But not completely. Something was stopping them both from doing so. She had an idea what the problem was on her side, couldn't say and perhaps didn't want to know what it was on his. But she couldn't ever trust him completely until he trusted her with what was inside his head and heart.

She didn't know how much longer she could endure this tug of war with him — and her heart.

"Lacey?"

She glanced up. "Yes?"

"I asked if I could fix you a glass of tea while I had the pitcher out for your daddy and me," Rachel said.

"Oh. Sure, thanks."

Her mother busied herself with the routine. After she had poured three glasses, instead of taking two of them to the upstairs sitting room, however, she marched to the table, slapped a couple of paper napkins under them, and sat down rather determinedly in a clear invitation for Lacey to join her there.

Lacey sank into a chair kitty-corner from Rachel, eyebrows raised in question.

Her mother got right to it. "I'm sorry about sendin' those computers back today. I shouldn't've done it, should've let you make that decision yourself, and I wanted you to know that."

"It's all right, Mother," Lacey said. She picked at the edge of the bandage on her hand. It seemed a million years ago that she'd injured it at this very table. "You must have been pretty worried about taking delivery on all those computers if you thought I'd be abandoning work on the center. I wouldn't leave you and Daddy in the lurch, believe me. Don't worry another minute about it."

"That's it!" Rachel's palm slapped the tabletop, making Lacey jump and bringing her head up.

"Mother, what is it?"

"I'll thank you not to humor me again, Lacey Jane McCoy! I won't say I haven't done anything to deserve it, but I am tryin' to understand why you still want to turn this house into a girls' center!"

Lacey sank back in her chair, her weariness of this morning returning tenfold. "After I told you about Nicolai's treatment of me, Mother, how could you not know how much setting this center up means to me?"

"I realize that. But you were also doin' it mostly to keep your father and me in this house, weren't you?" Rachel countered. "And it just seemed to follow how you're going to be settled out on the Double R soon, which means we'd be on our own again and would have to look to what we wanted to do once you're married. Because we don't want to stay in this house."

"You don't?" Lacey asked, dumbfounded. Was it not simply Will but her mother, too, that she was out of sync with? "But when we talked about it, you said there was no way you and Daddy could sell this house."

"Well, not for what it's worth, certainly," Rachel said tartly. "I was talkin' to your daddy last night, and I said I thought surely we could get a fair amount of money, more 'n enough to buy a nice little place and put away the rest. It'd make sense, don't you think?"

For several moments, Lacey could only stare at her mother in stunned silence.

"I don't understand, Mother," she said at last. "I simply don't understand. I thought this house was important to you, the last status symbol you had now that I'm no longer America's Cinderella."

"Well, it surely was nice to live here when you were. I'll admit I enjoyed the luxury — and, I'm ashamed to admit, feelin' superior to the other ladies around town."

Rachel's pale complexion pinkened. "But now that you're *not* married to a rich count . . . well, stayin' in a house like this when it's not affordable seems plain stupid. Your daddy and me, we've never been ones to live beyond our means, eating caviar on a pizza budget, as your daddy would say. Not when pizza is actually what suits him better. And me, too," she added a trifle defiantly.

Lacey continued to sit there in what she was sure was slack-jawed amazement. This was a side of her mother she'd never seen. Of course, she'd never seen the side of her mother which had been so prevalent since Lacey's return — the holding-onto-the-past-with-both-hands, unable-to-accept-the-future, unhappy-with-her-lot side. Although there had always been shades of those characteristics in her mother's personality, Lacey knew her own failed marriage and return to Abysmal in disgrace had magnified those traits in Rachel.

So what had caused *this* change of stripes?

"What's different from yesterday that would change your mind, Mother?"

Rachel fiddled with the edge of her napkin for a minute, eyes downcast. "I know I did you wrong by talkin' to Nicolai, and that it brought a powerful lot of trouble on all our heads. I felt terrible about it. But then it seemed almost like a wish come true how things turned around, with Will proposing. I'll grant it concerned me at first, even if I had a woman's intuition that you two had feelings for each other."

"You did?" Lacey blurted out, wondering what exactly her mother's instincts told her that Lacey was still trying to figure out herself. "How?"

"You could just tell. Oh, I know you were angry with him when he kissed you at the Summer Fling. And I heard about the quarrel you had outside the tack and feed. But when you announced your engagement, it seemed to me that everything was going to work out after all."

She raised her eyes, and Lacey could see they'd filled with tears again. "It hasn't, though. Last night when you came inside after Will left, I could tell you were desperate unhappy about something, and I thought maybe it was because you were worried what would happen to your daddy and me in this house. Then this morning the mix-up with the computers happened. . . . Honestly, Lacey, all I wanted to do was to help! And now, I thought you'd be happy to know you wouldn't have to worry about things here and could start fresh with Will, but it's plain to see you're as unhappy as ever."

With a sigh, Lacey squeezed her mother's hand. "I appreciate your wanting to help, Mother. But . . . but *you* never stopped working after you married Daddy, at least until I was born, and even after that you always kept the books and ran the finances for Daddy's business. So why would you expect me to give up the girls' center after marrying Will and just live the life of leisure?"

"I didn't expect you to," Rachel contradicted. "I just thought you'd move out to the Double R and be a part of that with Will. Be a part of the dreams he's buildin' on, and bringin' your own into the mix — like your girls' center — so they become your dreams together."

Rachel went on hastily, "It's not that we don't appreciate what you've done to help us not have to go through too many changes. We do. It's just that now it's time for us to do for ourselves."

Lacey shook her head, thoroughly perplexed. "I still don't get it. I mean, yesterday you were wanting to hold on to the past. And now you're willing to just go with the flow?"

"Well, yes." Her mother's blush grew even deeper. "Hank . . . your daddy . . . he's been real patient with me gettin' used to this whole situation and the changes to our lives. I haven't been at my best, I know — sometimes I've been downright unreasonable.

But thankfully we've been able to talk about it and work it out, so we could come back around to what's really important to us. With you goin' off to make your life with Will, your daddy and I needed to look at what was going to be right for just us two."

She gave an embarrassed laugh, and Lacey had to wonder only a second what it was about. "I'll have to say, it's been kind of exciting, planning together. I haven't felt anything like this in years, sort of 'you and me against the world,' you know?"

She regarded her mother with new perception. The two of them had never gotten along very well; where Rachel was concerned, Lacey had always felt she fell far short of doing the right thing. Now, Lacey saw that her mother really had been trying to give her daughter the support and advice she thought would help. The trouble was, it was difficult for Rachel to let go of control over the people in her life and just trust. Trust herself, mostly.

It wasn't easy to think about, but it occurred to Lacey that she was a lot like her mother in that respect. Yet her mother had been able to get past her issues to renew that sense of trust and taking risks, and now it seemed she had it all — along with a good man at her side.

It was how Lacey had felt briefly with Will. So why was she running so hard from experiencing such a feeling again? What was wrong with her that she'd push away something that seemed so right?

Lacey was silent, thrown into a sudden turmoil. Her mother must have sensed some of her conflict, however. "What is it, honey?" Rachel asked softly.

She couldn't tell the truth, mainly because she didn't know what the truth was at this moment. Swallowing past the lump in her throat, Lacey focused on a drop of condensation running down the side of her glass, and said as honestly as possible, "I think I was too hasty, getting engaged to Will."

"Has that been what's worrying you?"

Lacey nodded jerkily. "That — and telling you."

"Oh, honey." Rachel folded Lacey's hand between her two. "Truly, neither your daddy or I would ever want you to go into another marriage where you weren't happy! Do you want to call off the engagement?"

"No . . . maybe . . . oh, I don't know!" She knew that would invite so many more complications, including the possibility of Nicolai finding out and pursuing her again, but how much longer could she let the fear of what he might do dictate how she lived her life?

"Then you must take your time to know for sure," Rachel said. "Don't worry about your daddy and me. We'll figure out something to do about this house and the resource center. You're welcome to stay with us as long as you like. All we want is your happiness."

With one hand, she brushed back Lacey's hair, tugging gently so she had to lift her chin and look her mother in the eye. "But the choice of how you find it has got to be yours."

Was it? Lacey wondered. She, too, had been trying to control the people and events around her since her return. She had thought she was seeking her happiness, had promised herself she would. And she had, to a great degree, by pursuing her girls' center.

But now she realized she'd also devoted a lot of time and effort to trying to make others happy, believing she knew better than they what that was. In a way, she was not so very far from being like, not her mother, but Will.

On that thought, Lacey slid out of her chair and dropped to her knees in front of her mother to rest her head on Rachel's lap as she hadn't since she was a little girl.

"Oh, Mom, I've been so stupid, tryin' so hard to keep you in this house." Tears filled her own eyes and spilled over onto her mother's skirt. "I only wanted to make you happy."

"Lacey, you can't make another person happy." Rachel stroked her hair. "I — I did have a hard time comin' to grips with the situation when you came back to Abysmal, and I want to say right now I'm deeply sorry for puttin' my feelings on you like I did. You sure enough have shown me a few things about myself since you came back."

"I have?" Lacey mumbled. Hadn't Will said something like that to her, too?

"Oh, yes. You came back a whole different woman than the girl who left here. You're so strong and sure of yourself, and with a conviction of purpose, too. I've had to get to know you all over again." She lifted Lacey's face between her hands, and looked down at her with loving eyes. "That's why I'm so sure you'll find a way to make your girls' center a go no matter what. And your daddy and I'd still like to help, if you'll let us."

Lacey gave her a watery smile. "Let you! Just try not to!"

Pushing forward onto her knees, she

wrapped her arms around her mother, who hugged her back with all her heart.

"Well!" Lacey sat on her heels. "I'm sure Daddy's wondering where his iced tea is."

She picked up the perspiring glass and carried it to the foyer, trying not to think about what to do regarding Will and their sham engagement. Somehow, the thought of calling it off made her feel like she had a pit in her stomach a mile deep.

She recognized it as fear.

No! Stopping in her tracks, Lacey gripped the baluster at the foot of the stairs with one hand. She didn't want to feel this way any longer, afraid and uncertain and unhappy. She had promised herself when she left Nicolai that she wouldn't — she couldn't live that way.

She made herself take a deep breath and concentrate. What was she afraid of? And what *would* make her happy? Lacey asked herself.

The answer to the second question came to her first, as it had before in this very spot: to live her life as herself, to be accepted for herself. To be loved for herself.

To love freely, as herself.

And in that, it wasn't Nicolai who controlled her. Because what held her back was her own fear of trusting, of taking a risk —

and of being vulnerable. But unless she let go and took that risk, she would never know the kind of joy she needed to be happy and fully alive.

With a clarity of thought she'd never experienced before, Lacey knew she'd pass up her chance with Will if she didn't face those fears. With all her heart, she wanted to be free of them. Free to love again.

It meant letting go and trusting, even in the face of fear.

She had to do it. Because until she did, Nicolai would have won, for she would still be a victim of his abuse.

Legs shaking, Lacey mounted the stairs to the sitting room, where her father was watching TV. He barely glanced up when she handed him the tea.

"Would you believe the luck?" he said. "I found an old episode of *Gunsmoke* to watch!"

Lacey had to laugh. She patted her father on the shoulder. "Of all the extravagant furbelows that came with this house, I think you like the satellite dish most of all."

"That I do," Hank said, reaching up to grasp her hand, eyes still riveted on the screen. "I tell you, Texas hasn't seen men the likes of Marshal Dillon in a long time, has it?"

"Oh, I don't know about that," she murmured, gazing down at the gentle eyes set against his strong features. "I was wondering, Daddy — could I borrow the pickup?"

That brought his attention up. "Sure, darlin'. Any place special you're headin'?"

Beyond the pale and out into the wilderness, she almost answered. But she had to keep her courage up. Still, it helped to know she had the support of her father who, as with her mother, continued to let her find her way on her own. It took a rare sort of man to do that.

And there was a certain one she hoped she was right about.

"Oh, I don't know," she answered. "Can't I just be going for a drive?"

"Once upon a time you would've complained there was no place to drive *to* in this little town," Hank said on a chuckle, stretching out one leg so he could get into his jeans pocket for the keys.

Funny her father should use that expression. *Once upon a time.* The age-old beginning to every fairy tale. It wasn't once upon a time, though. It was now — and now was her time. But only if she seized the day.

Her pensiveness must have shown in her lack of response.

"Should I wait up?" Hank joked, but she

saw the concern in his eyes.

She squeezed his shoulder. "No. I'm going to be just fine."

With a trusting nod, he kissed the back of her hand before letting her go.

CHAPTER ELEVEN

Will leaned back against the side of the galvanized stock tank, the water lapping pleasantly around his waist. The night wind blowing unhindered across the bald plain felt as hot and dry as it ever had, making the water in the stock tank that much more refreshing.

He didn't do this enough, he decided then and there. He must drive past this tank ten times a week, and he never stopped longer than to check and make sure the windmill that pumped the water into the tank was still working properly. He was always too busy, had too much to do, to take much more of a pause.

Well, that was about to change.

Starting right here, right now, he was going to cut himself more slack time and hand over even more of the regular-type duties to Lee or Yancy. In fact, Will had just about come to the conclusion that someone had clobbered his brother with a gung-ho hammer, because Lee seemed energized and revitalized by the ranch responsibilities he'd been given, even in addition to his work at the tack and feed. He'd actually started worrying that Kid Brother might be working too hard, as if trying to make up for something. Or running away from it.

Will shook his head at the irony. Whatever the situation was, he fully intended to let Lee figure it out for himself.

An engine sounded in the distance, and without looking around he wondered who'd follow him out here tonight. Someone with a whole lot of guts, since he'd been ornery as an old cayuse at supper. Probably Lee, who'd put the idea about the stock tank in his head this evening, of a fashion. After the third time Will had bit off a ranch hand's head for some trivial thing that had or hadn't happened that day, Lee had pretty much told him where he and his surly attitude could go. Seeking slightly cooler environs than suggested had been Will's idea.

He heard the engine kill and a door slam. Yup, it'd be just like his brother to come out under pretense of giving him an I-told-you-so just to serve up another heaping helping of his cowboy advice to the lovelorn.

Well, Will wasn't in the mood for it. Not that he didn't deserve Lee's tongue-lashing or might not get something out of his counsel. He was simply done with talking today, especially about Lacey McCoy.

Thinking about her, however, he had a lot to get done yet. And it was proving frustrating.

He scooped a handful of water and slapped it on the back of his neck. Had heaven ever made a more mystifying creature? One minute she was looking up at him like he'd just lassoed the moon for her, and the next she was all for telling him where to shove it now that he had.

But he knew he had to take his share of the blame, that being how his inclination for thinking he knew what was best for people sometimes provoked such reactions, especially in Lacey.

Which disturbed him. He'd told her he was done coming to her rescue, and yet today he'd given in to impulse again — dropped everything to attend her in her time of trouble. He didn't know what it was about her that made him want to play Prince Charming, particularly when she'd forbidden anyone from taking that role. He only knew he wanted to win her trust, and his determined can-do way of proceeding

246

had always accomplished what he'd needed to before.

Except once.

"Hello, Will," came a voice behind him. Light and lilting it was, like a spoken song. And definitely not Lee's.

Will whipped around so fast the breeze caught his straw Stetson and took it clean off his head and into the water. He had just enough of a glimpse of Lacey's equally startled face before he swam over to snatch the hat up in case another gust came along and he lost it for good.

He shook the water off it before setting the hat back on his head. " 'Lo, Lacey," he said with a nonchalance that sounded as forced as a watermelon through a keyhole. "Beautiful evening," he added just as lamely.

"Yes," she answered without a bit of awkwardness. "I was just thinking, what a nice night for a swim. I always favored this spot in high school, in case Lee never told you."

"Really?" he drawled. "I'm surprised you'd even consider coming out here for a dip when you can practically fall out your back door into your own Olympic-size pool."

She hooked a lock of golden hair behind her ear, eyes downcast. "Actually, I didn't come out this time for the swimming opportunity." She paused. "Lee told me I'd find you here."

"Did he now?" Will wasn't sure whether he'd kill or kiss his brother when he saw him next, but then he guessed that would depend upon why Lacey was looking for him.

She seemed not in the least bit of a hurry to enlighten him on the subject as she climbed the ladder on the side of the tank to the narrow platform he'd had one of the hands rig up a few years ago for occasions such as this. She wore some kind of gauzy skirt. With a gracefulness he had admired before, she slid out of her flat-heeled shoes and sat so her feet dangled in the water.

Will turned so he faced the side of the tank, forearms propped on the platform next to her.

"Any . . . particular reason you were looking for me?" he said with the slightest croak in his voice. Like a frog jumping to do her bidding.

She concentrated on the swish of her feet through the dark water, making it swirl up against his flank in the most distracting way. "I wanted to let you know I'd talked to Jenna."

Will forgot about his awkwardness for the

moment. "And is everything okay?"

"It took a while to get a hold of her at the friends of Carla's where she's staying for now — it seems Carla's boyfriend wasn't serious about having her cousin move in. But yes, everything's okay . . . for now. She's pretty closemouthed about the situation. I figure that's because she's feeling a little humiliated at having to live off of strangers, and she's not wanting to give anyone the chance to talk her out of still trying to make a go of it."

She stuck out her lower lip pensively, and Will thought that, with the moonlight making a halo out of her golden hair, she looked like a lonesome angel. "But I think that's partly because she's trying to be brave. I told her what I'd told you I would."

"And?"

Now she looked not so much lonesome as disheartened. "She didn't have much to say in reply. I don't think she's used to having someone say they care." Her hands twisted together in her lap. "I — I hope I made an impression on her."

"I know you did, Lacey," Will reassured her.

"From here on out, though, it's up to her," she said staunchly. "I guess that's what worries me most, though — Jenna being on her own in a strange city, with virtually no support system, to figure out what will make her happy — and not just about her notions of fairy-tale romance."

She shivered suddenly, as if from a chill. "I get so scared inside for her when I think about it."

The quiet anguish in her voice was heart-rending. "Why?" he asked gently.

"Because I *know* what it's like to feel so alone — alone without anyone to understand."

Will put his hand over her two as they lay clutched in her lap. "But Jenna's not alone — she has you, even if you're not right there with her. And you're not alone anymore, either, Lacey. You have your parents and friends."

She shook her head in denial. "But for all the people around me, sometimes I feel more alone than ever. Oh, I appreciate my parents' support, and Lee is simply . . . Lee. Only I wonder sometimes if there's no one I can trust to completely understand who I am and what I need."

Will didn't hesitate a second in responding. "You can trust me, Lacey."

She drew her hands out of his grasp with a deliberateness that shot the hurt clear through to his core. "That's just it, Will — I don't know whether I can. I don't know any more about the person *you* are or what *you're* like inside than the rest of Abysmal. You keep your thoughts and feelings protected under lock and key, practically with chains of iron."

He was compelled to defend himself. "I think I've shown I've got a heart inside this tin chest. What about at the dance — or how we announced our engagement?"

"Yes, those well-orchestrated 'scenes,' " she murmured. "You said yourself how they were staged to have a certain effect, with very little risk."

She had him there. "So, are you sayin' you want me to be more like Lee, a man who'd eat his heart out over a woman in front of the whole town?" Will set his jaw. "Well, that's Lee's way, to wear his affections on his sleeve. It's not mine, though. And I'll make no apologies for that."

Lacey's response was a subdued "I see" and to pull her feet out of the water as she braced her palms on the platform. She was leaving, he realized, and something in her manner clued him in that she was going without getting what she'd come out here for. From him.

Reflexively, he reached out to detain her with his fingers around her ankle. She went

251

stock-still, like a wild animal sensing the clear-and-present danger of a predator.

He hated that he aroused such a reaction in her! He didn't understand what he did to make her so wary and afraid and defensive, even given her admissions of feeling vulnerable and powerless — and her judgments of him as Iron Will Proffitt.

"I'm not made of iron, Lacey, I can assure you of that without an iota of doubt," he said in a low voice. "How could you not know that, the way you set me off with barely a look."

She looked down at him with regret. "Yes, we both certainly have a way of bringing *those* feelings out in each other. But you must have realized today how there's something missing. I need more from you, Will."

So she'd said — she needed him to understand her completely. Well, he was trying, and getting pretty frustrated at not seeing where he was coming up short!

This wasn't in his experience, either. Whenever he'd come up against a problem in his life — be it the threat of the ranch going to pot under his father's management or fighting to bring that ranch back to prosperity or helping his brother get his life on track after a busted-up love affair — Will had been able to tackle it head-on, and so

252

had very little doubt about his ability to handle whatever came his way —

Except once. *I need more than you can give me, Will Proffitt.* The words had rung in his head for years, and perhaps always would. For when it came to women, Will Proffitt was as helpless as a two-day-old kitten.

No! Not with Lacey. He couldn't fail with Lacey.

He stared into her yearning green eyes. She was wanting to trust him — not that he would understand, though, but that he had it in him to give her what she needed. He told himself she must believe enough already that he could give that to her, or she wouldn't have come out here in the first place tonight. He took heart in that.

She was right, though; it wasn't enough. He wouldn't be satisfied with only part of her trust, just as she wouldn't be satisfied not trusting completely. But to win that trust he would have to give her his first — his complete trust.

He didn't know if he could go there. Didn't know if he wanted to find out for sure that he couldn't give a woman what she needed.

Although Lacey remained frozen in his grasp, Will knew he'd better come up with something pretty quick if he didn't want to see her walk away again, perhaps for the last time.

It was hard to know if he should even try. He didn't think he'd be able to take another failure. Especially not with Lacey. Because here was a woman who, almost more than love, needed to know she could trust. Somehow, he knew if he turned away from the appeal in her eyes, he'd never feel a complete man ever again in his life.

Will cleared his throat. Then again. Finally he said, "I'm not completely ignorant of what you went through with the breakup of your marriage, Lacey. Because I was married once myself. And when the relationship went south, it was the most confidence-shaking, pride-pulverizing, wound-licking experience of my life."

From the look on her face, he could have knocked her over with a feather. "I had no idea, Will," she breathed. "I mean, I suspected something had happened, but no one was talking."

"And you assumed they were too scared to, right?" he said dourly. Even now, his pride was taking a beating. "Or I'd have their head on a platter with fixin's."

She had the decency to blush. "I . . . I would like to hear what happened. If you'd like to tell me," she said with total earnestness.

He felt about as comfortable with the subject as he would finding himself in close confines with a rattler. But figuring he had little left to lose at this point, Will gave a curt nod and plunged in.

"Mary Ann was from Dallas, someone I met at a beef conference five years ago. We struck it off, and it kind of grew from there. I won't go into details other than to say it seemed right for us to marry, and I fully intended for it to last."

"But sometimes life — and love — doesn't go that way, does it?" Lacey murmured.

"You got that right," he said ruefully, settling forward, arms crossed on the wooden platform. "Anyway, we tied the knot and she moved out to the Double R — probably the first big snag in the marriage. She was used to the city, bein' within spittin' distance of her friends and family. I never denied her when she wanted to go see 'em, would drive her to Amarillo myself to put her on a plane. But I rarely went with her."

He waylaid any criticism Lacey might make by adding, "Ask any rancher around and he'll tell you there's no such thing as pickin' up on a whim and jauntin' off to the city. It's a full-time, round-the-clock job."

Will knew he must be scrupulously truthful, however, or the point of this confession would be lost. "On the other hand, I'll admit I was workin' pretty hard, harder than I had to. Same as I always have. It's just been my way since I was eighteen. Oh sure, no one made me work like a demon then, although even now I can't say I'm sorry I did. The Double R was on the brink of failure when I took over, and once it started prospering, it brought a lot of business to Abysmal, helped keep the town from turnin' into a ghost of itself like so many Panhandle towns did in those days."

He paused, taking a moment to gather the courage to admit this last part. He had to come completely clean, though. "But I didn't need to work as hard as I did once I got married. I'll be the first to own I started working harder to keep from havin' to think about what was goin' wrong with my marriage, even while I tried to find ways to make Mary Ann happy. I gave her free rein to remodel the ranch house, sort of to make it more hers, you know? I got the men I'd grown up with and worked with to come out with their wives and girlfriends to get to know her. Only it seemed the more I did, the more unhappy she got, and I'd be lyin' if I didn't tell you it so frustrated me I closed up to her. But I truly was doin' my best to provide for my wife and give her what she needed, and since workin' hard was what had brought me results before, then that was my way of tryin' to solve the other problems I had."

He didn't like how his words resounded with self-righteousness, or at least seemed to, to his ears. Apparently, Lacey caught the strain of his meaning, because she said, "I believe you, Will, that you were doing your best, and with the best intentions."

It helped to get the last part out. "Yeah well, I guess Mary Ann didn't think so. She left me. Walked out without a backward look."

He spread his hands, trying for casualness, feeling anything but. He felt as exposed as he would if he walked down Main Street in nothing but his B.V.D.s, and he understood more than he ever had Lacey's fierce need to protect her privacy about her personal tragedy. But there was no other way to tell his story except in the baldest of terms. "Oh, I've come to realize that while I certainly own a good share of the fault for the marriage goin' bust, she shared responsibility, too. I'm a hard case sometimes, but I think you can get me to concede to a wrongdoin' if I've done it. 'Cept she didn't give me the chance."

"Did you ask for one?" she asked without a bit of sympathy.

Will recognized his own device, used on her so many times. "No," he said tersely. "No, I didn't."

Yes, pride was a powerful thing in him.

And Will struggled mightily with what to say next, how to say it, because it was the most pride-shattering admission of all. "Every single soul in town knew she'd left me, though they weren't privy to why, and I wasn't inclined to enlighten them. That's what earned me the nickname Iron Will Proffitt. Without any explanation as to what really happened, people tended to believe the worst. *You* pretty much believed the worst — that I was this control freak cattle baron who had to run the show from start to finish and completely on my terms. The thing is, maybe you've got the right of it, in a way."

"I do?"

With all he had in him, Will struggled not to pull back from the truth right now. Somehow he knew if he did, he'd lose his chance with Lacey forever.

"Yeah, you do. Because I've come to see that what I wanted Mary Ann to need from me was only what I was comfortable giving

— my name, my position in the community, financial security. My power to make things happen. But not my attention, my support. Not . . . myself."

Done at last, he tipped his head back, eyes closed, curious to be feeling a kind of freeing relief. He had never told anyone the full story. In fact, he had probably never fully admitted to himself his faults and failings, and it was because he'd always held his emotions in, as Lacey — and Lee — had so bluntly told him. Likely his life would be a whole lot different right now if he'd done this sooner. Still, he wasn't one to beat himself up for past transgressions, although he could do a little more learning from them.

And what came to him right now was that if he hadn't done this before, it was because he hadn't risked losing so much.

He wondered if Lacey realized that.

She apparently had some sense of his struggle, for she said, "I know how hard it was for you to tell me that, Will, and I want to let you know, I'm honored that you did."

He swallowed with difficulty. Her appreciation meant a lot to him. And, he realized, made the hell he'd just gone through worth it.

"No harder than it was for you to tell me

about Laslo's abuse," he said gruffly.

She gazed out into the night, suddenly seeming a million miles away. He'd noticed before how she did that — withdrew into herself at the mention of Laslo.

She'd said that before, about how alone she felt at times. He realized he'd felt the same way for most of his life, mostly because he'd always had to be the one in charge, in control, and that had caused him to hold himself separate from those who depended upon him to be strong.

Lacey had had to be strong, too, although for different reasons. Stronger, in fact, than he'd had to be, for she'd been so much more vulnerable, had had to fight her way back from a position much more susceptible to attack.

"So you see, that's why I've been so unpredictable with you, Will," she explained. "I've felt like I could get only so close to you before I needed to protect myself because I didn't know whether I could ever allow myself to —" her voice roughened and she took a second to clear her throat "— to open up and completely trust a man. Or let myself l-love one. I just learned very well from Nicolai Laslo how love makes you vulnerable, and how many ways it can be used against you."

Her confession done, she hugged herself, almost as if she were trying to keep out the world so it wouldn't hurt her anymore. Or to hold in some longing which persisted despite what she'd gone through.

Will ached for her, ached for himself, too. The wounds ran deep in them both, but they had survived by building walls of protection around them. And for that they paid a price.

He felt regret, as well, although that was mostly for Lacey. Because he knew it would take her somehow regaining that youthful vision of true love forever and ever, to come all the way back from the hurt she'd suffered. But since he had been there himself, he knew how impossible it would be for either of them to ever believe in such a tall tale again.

"We're certainly a pair, aren't we?" he said quietly.

"Meaning?"

"Oh, that the personal ordeals we've been through have made us stronger, and there's a certain pride and conviction that comes from knowing you're a survivor. But our trials've also turned us into realists, which doesn't much make you popular because people don't want to hear from you that there's no such thing as a fairy-tale happy ending."

"But do we know that for sure, Will?" Lacey studied him for a long moment before going on with an enigmatic air, "Maybe . . . maybe it's not what people endure that provides the measure of their strength. Maybe it's continuing to step into the new, unfamiliar and dangerous territory of what each of us *hasn't* experienced is what makes us strong, because braving the unknown takes so much trust. And it's only by continuing to risk trusting that you even have a chance at any kind of happy ending."

Will frowned. "Yeah? Well, all I know is you can't make somethin' happen that's not going to happen."

Lacey continued to look at him strangely.

"And all I know is that staying in the place I'm at isn't working at all. And going back is not an option."

Before he could react, she placed her hands on either side of his face and bent to kiss him.

Chapter Twelve

She loved Will. She knew that fact to the bottom of her feet. Oh, to know she could still trust, could still love was part of it. But to love a man such as this, who had raised in her all her greatest fears and helped her face and conquer them one by one, as she had hopefully had a hand in helping him with his.

Tears sprang to her eyes and Lacey gave a small sob of relief — and thanks. This feeling was worth all the loneliness, all the hurt and pain — that which she'd endured and would endure.

"Lacey, I'm sorry I made you cry," Will muttered.

"No, I'm not crying about that."

"Then why?" he demanded.

She still had some fears left, it seemed. "I just . . . I've never felt anything so good. So right."

■ ■ ■ ■

They'd finally left the stock tank after Will dried himself off, and now, stretched out on the bench seat of the cab extension with Lacey snuggling against his chest, Will had to admit he was feeling well nigh on the best he ever had in his life.

There was something about being able to give a woman what she needed that did that to a man.

He felt a pinprick in his own elated satisfaction. He was engaged to this particular woman. On the surface, it would seem there wasn't much to debate on the subject. Except they both knew it wasn't real.

So what was real? What had just happened between them — *that* was real, as real as it got. And because it was, he owed it to Lacey — owed it to them both — to honor that experience by following through with his pledge, even if it had been for show, to give her his name and protection. And while he was at it, maybe he'd make a few of her other dreams come true, like funding her resource center.

Except Lacey had said several times she didn't want Prince Charming to come riding up on a white horse and rescue her.

She didn't need a man to take care of her. Or protect her. So what did she want — and need — from him, especially now?

He would do it, if he only knew.

"I'd better get you home," Will whispered. "I don't want to worry your parents by keepin' you out to all sorts of hours."

Lacey cuddled closer to him, obviously not in any hurry. "Oh, they don't know I'm with you, first of all. But I think they'd figure it was all right since in their minds we're engaged."

"And in your mind?" he asked before thinking, which was getting to be a habit where she was concerned. Although maybe that's what it was going to take, for she lifted up on one elbow, bringing her into the shaft of moonlight shining in through the window. Her face seemed illuminated from the inside. Her skin positively glowed, and he couldn't help hoping it was because they both now knew each other better than anyone else. And because they had talked about everything, she might be feeling what he was right now.

Her voice was perfectly calm, however, as she said, "We both knew, Will, when we decided to pretend we were engaged that it was to keep Nicolai from coming to Abysmal. At the time, it seemed the best choice.

Maybe my only choice. But now . . ."

"Now?" he echoed, trying not to anticipate her next words while still bracing for them as he would a kick to the stomach by a bull.

"Now . . . Will, I want you to know I can never thank you enough for what you've given me tonight. You trusted me enough to tell me everything. No matter what happens, I'll cherish what we shared for the rest of my life."

Her green eyes were unfathomable. "That's why I won't make a mockery of it by continuing this charade of an engagement."

His breath left him as if he had indeed taken a hoof with a ton of force behind it to the gut. He tried to hold on to the good in her words, but it was powerfully hard when all he heard was that, even after tonight, she wanted to end their partnership, which had made him feel whatever happened as a result was all worth it.

"So what do we do — cause another scene in the middle of Main Street to call it off between us?" he asked pointedly. "I'll admit I'm hard-pressed to come up with something that'll stick with that crowd considerin' how we carried on to convince them we were the real deal. I'm thinkin' it'll take nothin' less than a full-scale, no-holds-barred free-for-all. Not a tiff, not a spat, not a squabble, but a real mud-slinger, complete with yellin' and foot stompin' and accusations flung all over the place."

Hurt shone from her eyes. Well, he was hurt, too!

"We'll simply tell people we got carried away by the moment," Lacey said, sitting up. "The rest is between us."

"I agree." He pushed himself upright, too, cinching his towel a little tighter around his waist in a move he realized was purely because of his feeling vulnerable as a just-hatched chick. "But you know Abysmal. People will wonder who dumped who and why, and if the answer isn't practically printed in the *Times* and parsed up and down, they'll come up with their own theories. And believe me, they can come up with some good ones."

Realization came over her features. "I wouldn't make you go through that again, Will. Honest I wouldn't. You should know that by now."

"And don't you know by now I honestly would do about anything to keep your private business from being put under a magnifying glass and then broadcast all over creation," he said with exasperation. "I'm tellin' you, Lacey, the last thing you need is

Laslo gettin' wind of our engagement being broken and him comin' to town after you."

They locked gazes in a different version of one of their stare-downs. This one, Will realized, was again about stubbornness, again about a tussle of wills. Again about fears untold.

For that's when Lacey murmured, "Actually, I've been thinking that's exactly what I need."

Will wondered if he could remain calm. But then he'd had years and years of practice keeping himself under tight rein. Never had it been as difficult as now, however.

He ran a hand through his hair, trying to think logically. Trying to regain a sense of control of the situation, although he felt anything but. "Look, there's no rush to do anything at this point, especially since we both can't come up with a better solution right now. So let's just leave the matter as it is until we can think this through and not make another hasty decision."

"I don't know if I can do that, Will. I want to tell my parents, at least," she said with a determined air. "I don't want to continue misleading the people I care about."

And what about him? he wondered. Where did he fall in her estimation?

She must have sensed something of his

thoughts, for Lacey laid her hand on his arm, her thumb brushing the inside of his forearm in a way that made him wonder at the wisdom of letting himself know the rare pleasure of holding this woman in his arms. For he was instantly affected by her touch, instantly on that slippery slope of losing himself in her.

"Will, please," she said, "you know better than anyone else on this earth how hard I've fought to keep hold of my sense of self. And I'm anything but sorry we decided to pretend we were engaged. It was the best thing to do at the time. But please try to understand when I say I've got to continue following my instincts about how to handle things — between us, with my parents, even with the center. I — I promise I'll keep your concerns at the front of my mind every minute. But . . . I have to do what's right, and I may not know what that is again until I'm smack in the middle of a predicament."

"Like *this* predicament?" he asked.

She removed her hand. He knew she needed a little more patience and understanding from him right now, but for the life of him he couldn't give her the words of support she wanted. He was just plain fresh out of them, just as he was fresh out of ideas to solve her problem any better than she was proposing. He'd already made the mistake of jumping in and trying to move all the chess pieces around to make things right for everyone.

"Fine, Lacey," he said at last. "You do what you've got to do. Just remember I'm doin' what I've got to, too."

And difficult as it was, Will knew he had to do nothing at this point, even if it made him feel more a failure than he ever had in his entire life.

He saw her to her truck and handed her into it, catching a glimpse as he did so of her downcast face, like a lonesome angel. He almost dragged her back inside the dually, locking the doors behind them so they'd have to hash this out. Or so he could kiss her again and convince her in that way that it would be all right, they could work it out somehow in a way that met both their needs.

But he didn't. He couldn't mislead her, either. Not that he would, only he had a lot of thinking to do before he came up with a new plan.

Because while he was happy to have confronted his fear of not being able to give a woman what she needed, Will realized he had a new fear: that of not being the man Lacey needed in a happily-ever-after situation.

Lacey stepped out of the post office, barely acknowledging Hector Baker's greeting as he brushed past her, so intent was she on the envelope she held in her hand. The return address indicated it was from Austin. Within it, Lacey knew, was the answer to her request for government funding for her resource center.

She'd applied for other grants, but this was the big one. If she got funding from the State of Texas, she'd be able to use that to garner attention from other funding sources. Then she'd be able to pay off the loan with the bank and start running the center like a real nonprofit.

With shaking fingers, she tore open the envelope and unfolded the letter inside, reading quickly.

Phrases jumped out at her, certain words sticking in her mind and in her throat, too. Words like *regret* and *unfortunately* and *please try again next year.*

Dazed, Lacey slumped against the brick side of the building. She didn't know how long she must have remained in that position, but when she finally roused herself, the heat of the late-afternoon sun had seeped through her clothes, making her perspire and draining her of the rest of her energy.

She folded the letter, blinking rapidly. Yes, there was always next year. She mustn't let this setback get to her. She'd apply for more grants, and there was plenty of credit left on the equity line.

But not enough to keep them afloat for another year, especially in that house.

Her parents had put out feelers around town about selling the mansion, and the news that had come back had been discouraging at best: even pricing it in steal-of-the-century range, the house still stood out as an expensive piece of property for this little town. And even if someone did step forward to buy it, it still was quite a burden to maintain, as Lacey's parents had discovered.

She felt even more of a responsibility than ever to see the situation settled to everyone's benefit.

Some sixth sense made her look up. There, at the end of the street, was Will, getting out of his pickup in front of the tack and feed. He obviously hadn't seen her — or had, and chosen not to acknowledge her.

She could understand if he had. They'd been dancing around each other like this for a week. She had a sense that Will was no

closer to an idea on how to handle "breaking off" their engagement than she was,
although she'd taken her parents into her
confidence. She had to be truthful with
them; she owed it to them. Owed it to
herself.

She'd also explained the situation to Jenna
the last time she talked to the girl, which
had been over five days ago. Lacey still
didn't know why she'd felt compelled to tell
the girl, except perhaps to demonstrate to
her how there was nothing written in stone,
no action at this point which couldn't be
taken back.

Except there was no taking back what had
happened between her and Will. Lacey had
given him her trust, she'd given him her
heart. Because she loved him, she would
not be with him in anything but the most
honest of relationships. And this engagement wasn't honest.

Lacey clutched the crumpled letter to her
chest as she watched Will disappear inside
the tack and feed without a glance around,
pained by this distance between them after
the closeness at the water tank. They were
back to protecting their innermost feelings.
Oh, she understood why, for each of them
had been hurt so terribly in the past. You
didn't automatically throw down walls that

had been built to last. But she knew if she and Will were to have a chance, they both had to be able to expose that deepest part of themselves, the part that was so vulnerable and perhaps still healing, even when they were in conflict with each other. Most of all then, in fact. It was how trust grew, how fears were kept from destroying it. And she knew she must feel completely trustful with a man in order to be truly happy.

Or should she count her blessings at having been given the opportunity to find out what kissing was like with a caring, responsible, good man, even if neither of them might ever reach that level of trust with each other?

Was she a romantic fool for wanting the fairy-tale kind of love which seemed so complete and unconditional?

"Now what is that?" Hector Baker said, snapping Lacey out of her absorption. He stood in the doorway to the post office, shading his eyes as he peered down the street.

Lacey squinted at the large form advancing from the west side of town, but she couldn't make it out, either, what with the sun pitched directly at eye level and the heat mirages coming off the pavement.

"It's probably a semi carrying cattle on its

way to one of the ranches to pick up a load," she guessed aloud.

Squirreling his mouth around a jaw full of chaw, Hector shut one eye as if sighting down the barrel of a hunting rifle. "Naw, this ain't just one vehicle."

She took another look and saw he was right. In fact, it was a company of what looked like large trucks, cars and vans.

A tremor of fear spread through her.

"Looks like a military invasion," observed Old Man Wilkins, polishing his bifocals on his shirt before setting them back on his nose to get more of a gander from his position on the bench nearby. "Nope, I do believe —"

"It's them TV people again!" interjected Vernal Adams with the scoop. "See them antennas and satellite dishes? Now, why would they be comin' back to Abysmal so soon? Ain't nothin' happened in the week since they were here last." She gave Lacey a probing look. "Has it?"

Lacey didn't answer but moved forward ahead of the crowd of townspeople filtering onto the street from their various shops and stores along Main to watch in mute curiosity as the procession drew closer.

Until the lead car became recognizable. A buzz went up around her, which Lacey barely heard for the warning clanging in her ears.

It was a black Mercedes limousine. She had traveled in one like it countless times, for eight years had not ridden in any other make of vehicle, since Nicolai wouldn't deign to own anything but that status symbol among automobiles.

In the next instant a Vise-Grip took hold of her throat, so tightly no air could get through. She dragged at the collar of her T-shirt, trying to stay calm, trying to relax enough to get a breath. Just one breath.

The limousine came to a stop twenty feet away. The driver, dressed in stately black livery, moved with precision as he opened the passenger door.

Out stepped a tall, elegantly thin man in a perfectly tailored charcoal gray suit which exactly matched his distinguished-looking salt-and-pepper hair. Still, he tugged at each sleeve with an air of command, adjusting the drape as his deep-set eyes scanned the crowd. His skin was tanned, his straight nose patrician, his full mouth aristocratic.

He glanced slowly around the square, eyes appraising as a general evaluating a battlefield. Then they lit on her.

He walked forward, his gait exuding confidence and authority. The smile he flashed was pure white and perfect. He looked every inch the charming prince. Yet what was a prince without a princess for him to make happy?

Lacey kept her face completely blank, but inside she felt as if depth charges were sounding in her chest at a rate of a hundred a minute. Their message reverberated in her brain: *Show no emotion, not the flicker of an eyelash, not the twitch of a lip. Don't give him a single clue he can use against you.*

He stopped before her, and though his eyes seemed lit with delight, she knew from long, hard experience that behind them was a brain which never stopped scheming, never initiating a gesture that wasn't calculated down to the merest of movements.

"My dear Lacey, it's so good to see you again," Nicolai said warmly, taking her hands in his and holding her arms out as he gave her a head-to-foot appraisal. "And don't you look as charmingly unaffected and unpretentious as the day I met you! This quaint little town obviously agrees with you."

His eyes were trained like a hawk's on hers. In their depths was a coldness that went beyond dead.

She had to bite down on the inside of her cheek to keep from jerking away in revulsion. Any reaction, positive or negative, would be used against her in some way.

It was a wonder she escaped him once with her spirit intact.

"Don't I even warrant a hello?" he asked, gazing at her as if he had eyes only for her but as aware as she that they had an audience of nearly two hundred people. Plus the newspeople, whom out of the corner of her eye she could see scurrying to set up around the two of them so as to capture this tender — or hopefully, in their estimation, antagonistic — moment.

She needed to keep in mind she could use the media against Nicolai as well as he could against her.

"Hello . . . Nicolai," Lacey said, and decided to go on the offensive. "What brings you to Abysmal? You were always quite clear during our marriage you'd never set foot in . . . now how did you put it? Oh, yes . . . 'that no doubt aptly named little burg you hail from.' "

A nearly undetectable spark of anger leapt in the back of his eyes. "Actually, I am delighted to see how mistaken I was," he answered with just the right degree of genuineness. "In fact, I've come to ensure this dear city's proper place in history — by making your dreams come true, my dear."

The gall of the man! "The only way you could do that is to tell me you intend to turn around and take yourself and this circus you've brought with you back to wherever you came from and stay out of my life for good," Lacey said bluntly, uncaring for the moment of how her reaction might look to people. She simply couldn't stand by while he got away with his charade.

"It grieves me to see how uncharitable you've become toward me!" Nicolai said, dramatically pressing his hand to his pristine shirtfront. "Perhaps once you see whom I've brought you, you'll find some warmth in your heart for me."

With that, he beckoned toward the limo. The driver opened the door again, and from within the dark interior emerged a slim, elegant young woman dressed impeccably in a saffron-yellow business suit, her brunette hair pulled back in a sleek chignon. She, too, paused dramatically and from behind dark glasses surveyed the crowd gathered on the street as cameras clicked and videotape whirred. Then her eyes found Lacey, and she broke out in a girlish smile and waved her hand excitedly.

Lacey gaped, transfixed. "J-Jenna? Is that you?"

All pretense at sophistication fell away as

the girl tore off her glasses and flung her arms wide. "It's me, all right! Don't I just look like I could meet the queen? And it's all because of Nicky!"

CHAPTER THIRTEEN

Squeals of delight came from the throng, and Lacey recognized two of Jenna's friends, who ran to her and hugged her before exclaiming over her outfit.

Lacey spun on Nicolai in a blaze. "You low-down jerk! If you think you can use Jenna or anyone else to get to me, I swear I'll make you wish you'd never heard the name Lacey McCoy!"

"My dear Lacey, please!" Nicolai held up his hands. "I've done nothing of the kind. I merely contacted Jenna in Houston to ask her a few questions, and she told me how you'd talked to her of returning home. She's wanted to, you know — she simply needed a guiding hand." He gestured. "You see?"

Lacey turned. Jenna's father had stepped forward and stood half a dozen feet from his daughter. He hesitated, as did an abruptly sobered Jenna, before they came together, and he engulfed her in a bear hug which elicited a collective "awww" from the throng.

At the sight, Lacey's heart dropped to her knees. Oh, it wasn't that she wasn't glad for Jenna. She was thankful she'd returned to Abysmal, however it had come about. But finding the girl and bringing her home in a way which made Jenna's own dream of being someone special come true . . . it was a master stroke by Nicolai.

Then another thought hit her. If he'd found out from Jenna how Lacey had been in contact with her and why, then he surely knew by now about the girls' center.

She couldn't stand the idea that he would have even the slightest knowledge of that most cherished of dreams — that was, except for one other dream she held close to her heart . . .

Horrified, Lacey wondered if Jenna had revealed to Nicolai the real nature of her engagement to Will! She could only hope the girl had known to keep her counsel.

Right now, however, Lacey needed to take back control of herself and this situation with Nicolai.

Lifting the corners of her mouth in a reasonable approximation of a smile, she faced him. "Thank you, Nicolai, for providing that last little incentive needed to convince Jenna to come home and attend classes at my resource center in town. I'm sure she's told you all about it. It's my dearest hope that before they venture out into the big, wide and often brutal world, she and girls like her learn the skills needed to make the choices that are right for them and not have to depend upon others to take care of them. Oh, I nearly forgot to tell you!" Lacey affected surprise. "You'll be gratified to know it's because of your generous gesture toward my parents in building that grand mansion for them that we've had a place to set up the center. It's worked out perfectly, in fact, now that we've been able to make the modifications needed."

She wouldn't come right out and say it, but she hoped her implication that the reason she had been "scrabbling" for money, in Nicolai's words, was not to keep her parents in their home but to raise funds for a good cause.

Lacey waited, hoping she'd said enough to turn the crowd and media back to her side. Nicolai made noises of depreciation for his part in the project, but she could tell he hated having to give even the slightest ground to her. She didn't know if inspiring ire in him worked for or against her.

Or had she made any progress at all? For

just then Jenna hurried over, her unfamiliarity walking in high heels making her look like she was on stilts. "Oh, but I won't need to come to your center, Lacey," she said.

"No?" Lacey asked, confused. "But why not?"

"Because Nicky's sending me to college!"

It was another shot to the heart of Lacey's own aspirations for Jenna, but she kept her composure — with effort.

"How wonderful for you, Jenna!" she enthused, giving the girl a quick hug.

"You don't keep secrets very well, do you, young lady?" Nicolai said with false modesty, touching a fingertip to Jenna's nose. She grinned abashedly. Pain shot through Lacey's jaw as she clamped down on her molars to hold her anger in check. She was deathly out of practice, however, at hiding her emotions behind a mask, she realized.

"I'm afraid it's true, though," Nicolai continued. "I've enrolled her at one of the finest women's colleges on the East Coast, all expenses paid I believe is how you Americans so succinctly put it." He took Jenna's hand and held it up, as if showing her off, Pygmalion-like, and Lacey could see that was exactly what he was doing. "She'll be the first of America's Cinderellas — of course, after you, dear Lacey. You'll

284

always be first in everyone's heart — including my own."

He grasped Lacey's hand with his free one and held it aloft as well, and the cameras went off like a string of firecrackers.

Lacey thought she'd be sick. She wanted to give them a real photo op — jerk her hand away, grab Jenna's, and run as far away from this man as she could take them both. It took everything in her to keep from doing so; her resistance was running low.

But what on earth could he mean about Jenna becoming America's Cinderella?

"What are you talking about, Laslo?"

The question hadn't come from her. Lacey glanced around to find Will standing ten yards away, stance wide, Stetson pulled low on his brow, hands looking relaxed and loose at his sides, as if he were ready for a shoot-out. Certainly, if looks could have killed, Nicolai would have been a dead man then and there.

As it was, that flinty stare was enough to get Nicolai to drop both Lacey's and Jenna's hands.

"Ah, and you must be the distinguished Will Proffitt," Nicolai said, smooth as silk, but Lacey knew she was the only one there who recognized, when he ran a hand down his tie, the uncharacteristic nervousness in the gesture.

"Distinguished or otherwise, I am," Will said tersely. He walked, loose-hipped and unhurried, to Lacey's side, where he put an arm around her and snugged her up against his side in a gesture of conspicuous proprietorship.

She wished he hadn't done that. Not that she wasn't grateful, as always, for his support but she knew Nicolai, knew how to handle him, at least with enough skill to fend off his manipulative lunges for the throat if not strike a blow of her own.

But she *had* grown out of practice in dealing with such manipulations. Until now, she hadn't actually realized how bad it had been with Nicolai — or how much freer she felt with Will.

That was the other reason Lacey wished him away from here. She wouldn't be able to conceal her feelings for him, not entirely. And Nicolai would use them against her. When he did, she feared he'd succeed, too.

For while Will Proffitt had become her greatest strength, at this moment he was also her greatest weakness.

She could only try to divert Nicolai's attention.

"What *did* you mean about Jenna being America's Cinderella?" she asked him, evincing no outward reaction to Will's presence beside her, while pressing the back of her hand against the outside of his thigh in silent warning.

Her diversion seemed to work. She'd given Nicolai the opening he'd been angling after since he stepped out of the limo, she realized, for she caught the gleam of triumph in his eyes as he said, "Only that Jenna has been ever so candid in explaining to me your concept for a girls' resource center here in Abysmal."

He barely managed not to lift his upper lip in disdain at the name. "It sounded exactly like you, my dear, idealistic and noble — but as with so many noble aspirations, one needs marry idealism with action to bring them to fruition."

He made no pretense now of not playing to the crowd as he swung gracefully about, facing them. "That's why I've had my business people in New York draw up plans for a foundation to fund and open such centers all around the United States. In fact, I've already set up offices there and have pledged a million dollars toward the cause."

Lacey swayed with shock. Any previous bombshell he'd dropped in the past eight years was nothing to this one.

She fought with everything in her to keep

her composure. *How had he known?* She'd told no one but Will of her hopes in that direction!

But then, this sort of shrewdness was signature Nicolai. He had made a study of her for nearly a decade, had devoted his every effort to finding out what made her tick — with the precise aim of using that knowledge against her.

As he was doing right now, taking her dream away from her and putting it under his control.

She wanted to start centers in other cities! Granted, she hadn't the resources right now to fund even one here in Abysmal, but she would get there!

Will's fingers dug into her arm, not so much steadying her physically as emotionally. Yes, he was the only one who understood what this revelation from Nicolai meant to her. Will said not a word, however, and for that she loved him to pieces. The effort to remain silent must be costing him, too.

His support also gave her the perspective she needed, for Lacey realized suddenly this cause wasn't about her, any more than it was about Nicolai. It was about the thousands of girls out there, girls like Jenna who needed, as Nicolai had said, a guiding hand, challenging opportunities, and the reinforcement that they could make their own dreams come true.

And if Nicolai could provide that, then who was she to discourage him?

"C-congratulations, Nicolai," Lacey said numbly. "You'll be helping a lot of young women with your foundation."

"Oh, but I'm merely providing the muscle, so to speak. You, Lacey, are the soul of the machine."

"Me?" she was surprised into asking.

"Why, of course. Jenna thought you might call the foundation America's Cinderella for Girls. With your approval, of course. Without you at the helm, there's no foundation. After all, this is your concept — a concept —" he swept an arm around, taking in the whole of Main Street and its occupants "— far more reaching, it seems to me, than this worthy but limited venue. And you *are* America's Cinderella, the woman whom every girl in the United States dreams of becoming."

As if on cue, murmurs of approval drifted to her from the townspeople. Playing the moment for all it was worth, Nicolai spread his hands before her as if in deferral. "But I understand if your feelings toward me prevent you from accepting such an opportunity at my hand."

He touched Jenna's hair with seeming tenderness. "We've talked about the possibility, and Jenna, too, would understand if your vision for her is different from what I've offered her. But that is your choice."

If he had wanted to design a way to tear down her guard completely, he couldn't have succeeded more. A foundation — run by her. For one moment, Lacey submerged herself in the prospect: she would have the ability to bring in experts and consultants to develop curriculums, would have the manpower to gather statistics on which age groups responded to which approaches in learning and character building. Would have the clout to get her girls into the best programs at the best universities . . .

Such as with Jenna, who now stood looking at Lacey with a whole world of possibilities — a world of hope — in her eyes.

Yes, Lacey held a lot of power in her hand right now, for Nicolai's implication was that if she turned down this opportunity, she would be selfishly cutting off those possibilities for hundreds if not thousands of girls around the country, including Jenna.

And that's when Lacey saw what this whole act by Nicolai was about. It wasn't actually about him turning public sympathy back toward him and discrediting her. No, his aim was to show everyone — but mostly her — that only with his wealth and power and influence could she be America's Cinderella.

Oh, she couldn't care less about a title she'd never wanted in the first place, but how could she not seize this opportunity to use her notoriety to help hundreds of girls around the nation to develop and maintain their own sense of independence?

Then the irony of the situation hit her, for the question was, how *could* she do it? How could she compromise the very principles and freedom of choice in herself that she wished to foster in young women?

Some small movement from Will popped her out of her reverie, and she glanced up to see the concern in his eyes.

"So, just what are your conditions for Lacey takin' your offer?" Will abruptly asked Nicolai.

Lacey blinked in dismay. What was he doing?

"Why, I thought that was clear," Nicolai protested innocently. "Nothing. Nothing at all. As I said, this would be her foundation. It would be my greatest pleasure to see my ex-wife continue the fine work she's started here in Abysmal. She would have complete authority."

"Now, why'm I not convinced of that?" Will drawled.

Nicolai rubbed his chin, momentarily evincing perplexity. "Of course. I see where your objection might come from, Mr. Proffitt. Lacey *would* be required to move to New York to run the foundation, since that is where I've set it up."

Will apparently comprehended the matter just as it struck Lacey, for he returned levelly, "And that's what you want, isn't it? To get Lacey away from the support and love of all her family and friends again — or is it away from me?"

Nicolai met his gaze as evenly. "You're quite astute, Mr. Proffitt. I'll admit I've had such an objective in mind since learning of your precipitously announced engagement. My investigations since then have only confirmed my suspicions. Still, I was reluctant to make such information public and embarrass Lacey — or yourself, Mr. Proffitt."

"Oh, please, don't be bashful. You got somethin' to say, no point in beatin' around the bush about it," Will said mildly enough, but an angry flush painted the ridge along his cheekbones, which Lacey considered a bad sign, for she knew Nicolai would have noted it, too. "*If,* that is, you've actually got anything on me."

With a shrug that said *It's your funeral,* Nicolai turned to Lacey. "What I learned is that you've needed money to get your center off the ground. And that Mr. Proffitt is quite frankly the wealthiest and most powerful man in this corner of the world."

Now Lacey fought to contain her anger. "I am not a gold digger, Nicolai!"

"Oh, I wasn't suggesting you were! On the contrary, I had assumed the situation was quite the opposite, what with Mr. Proffitt's influence at your town's estimable banking institution and with the powers-that-be at city hall. After all, aren't such machinations business as usual around here?"

A rumble of indignation reverberated through the townspeople.

"Are you insinuating that I pressured Lacey into gettin' engaged to me or she wouldn't get the help she needed to start her center?" Will snarled. "Because you couldn't be further from the truth!"

Nicolai's midnight hair, shot through with silver, gleamed in the sun. His suntanned skin radiated health and well-being. Not a wrinkle, not a blemish, not a single imperfection marred face nor clothes nor presence. But never had Lacey seen a blacker, more devious soul.

For she almost knew his next words before they were out of his mouth: "My dear Lacey, tell me right now that it's always been your true intent and wish to marry Mr. Proffitt, and I'll be on my way without another word."

She stared at him. How neatly he'd maneuvered both of them into this position! And they had played right into his hand.

If she answered yes, she and Will were to marry, she handed Nicolai the most powerful weapon he could find to use against her: her own attempt at subterfuge, which he would expose and use to discredit both her and her aim. There'd be no stopping him then. He'd move on to Will, her parents, the whole of Abysmal!

She had fought this man for eight years to hold on to her integrity. She couldn't let him take it from her now!

Yet if she said she didn't intend to marry Will, then it as good as confirmed that she was emotionally unstable and hadn't known her own mind in divorcing Nicolai, which gave him the satisfaction of showing himself to be blameless in their divorce, since she wasn't about to reveal the thousands of humiliations she'd endured from him during their marriage which had driven her to leave him.

But she would endure a thousand more right now, gladly, if only to keep from telling Nicolai she wouldn't be marrying Will. Because in saying that, she'd humiliate him, too, cast aspersions and doubt on his reputation, in front of the whole town and, judging from the fervor of the newspeople, the whole world.

That was the real test of character Nicolai had put before her.

She would have given anything not to be in this position, but the damage was already done. She had no choice.

Staring into Will's eyes, she asked him to understand why she had to say what she must.

"We aren't getting married," Lacey said. She wouldn't compound the situation with more lies.

From behind her she heard a unified gasp of shock as if from a Greek chorus. She heard mumblings of "seemed awful strange, now that you mention it," and "never did see it myself . . . America's Cinderella and Iron Will Proffitt."

Will's face was ashen but composed. She couldn't begin to guess the first thing about what he was thinking, but he had to have realized how Nicolai had trapped them both, and how they must be very careful not to compound the error by giving him more ammunition to use against them.

Yet she couldn't stand to see him disgraced in front of everyone, with her as the cause.

"It's not what you think," Lacey said earnestly. "Really, it's not."

"Then please, do enlighten us all," Nicolai urged.

Her mind whirled, as she tried to calculate ten moves ahead the consequences of any further statement she might make, as if playing a game of chess.

"It . . . it's no one's business but mine and Will's," she finally said, knowing she would only fuel more speculation but unwilling to expose either herself or Will to another attack.

"Of course. It's entirely a private matter. Yet it remains you're not marrying the rancher, so can I assume America's girls will be able to count on you, Lacey?" Nicolai asked, not bothering this time to disguise the exultant note in his voice.

He understood her so well, perhaps better than she herself did at times, but never had it been more clear to her how he would always use that knowledge against her, to try to control her and tame her and bring her to her knees before him. She found, surprisingly, that it hurt, for she had once given this man her heart to hold in trust.

She could only be thankful she hadn't given him her true heart. But it seemed he wouldn't be satisfied until he got her soul. And *that* he'd never have.

In that moment, the answer came to her of what she must say.

She had opened her mouth when Will said, voice calm, gaze fast upon Nicolai, "I'll write a check right now for whatever you need to fund your center here, Lacey, no strings attached, no marriage, nothing."

"What?" Lacey asked.

"I know it's not a national foundation, but it's somethin'. Somethin' that might get you to stay."

Stunned, she could only gaze at him in disappointment. Didn't he see it wasn't about taking one offer or another, how he had just done to her what Nicolai had, asking her to choose, forsaking her heartfelt aim in order to achieve it?

She thought he understood that about her, was the one person on earth who could!

And now he'd put her in the most difficult position of all!

Tears filled her eyes, the hurt was so great.

"Will . . . I can't . . . I don't want . . ." She couldn't go on.

"A generous offer, Mr. Proffitt. Quite obviously, however, the matter seems already to have been settled," Nicolai said with a lift of his eyebrows. "Has it not, my dear Lacey?"

"It has not." Will placed himself between the two of them, and Lacey's stomach twisted with foreboding. Jenna paled and backed up a good five steps. "And she's not your Lacey, dear or otherwise."

Nicolai examined his manicure. "She's apparently not yours, either, Mr. Proffitt."

"More mine than she ever was yours," Will said, deadly low, his words reaching only Lacey's and Nicolai's ears. His meaning was clear.

And it got to Nicolai as Lacey had never seen anything affect him before. Dropping all pretense at nonchalance, he replied, voice dripping with scorn, "And as I can see, it came at quite a price to you."

What his next intention was, Lacey didn't know, but it took only the twitch of Nicolai's hand before Will was all over him, large fists grasping handfuls of that immaculate charcoal suit, as he brought his face to within in an inch of Nicolai's.

"You may be some kind of big shot in that

298

pint-size kingdom you come from, but this is my town. And here, you hold about as much sway as a fence post. For all your fine talk of doin' good and savin' Lacey from me, it's pretty clear to everyone you didn't come here with anything else in mind other than to see how much off her rocker you could make her seem for preferrin' a rough-actin' Texas rancher and this little town on the edge of nowhere to all your culture and fortune and fame."

Nicolai looked as if he would burst of anger in the next second, for Will had virtually summed up the situation in a nutshell. Yet with that canny sixth sense of his, which could shoot straight as an arrow to the heart of another's vulnerability, Nicolai answered, "Perhaps you're forgetting Lacey left here once because she hadn't found what she needed. Who's to say she won't again?"

Will's fingers turned white, and for a moment Lacey wondered if he would lose it himself and actually hit the other man. She didn't know what she'd do if he did. Given how hushed the crowd had become and how closely focused each camera was on the two men, she couldn't help feeling it would spell disaster not only for Will, but for the whole of Abysmal.

It was exactly what Nicolai wanted.

"Let him go, Will," Lacey ordered. "At once."

He moved not a muscle for a good five seconds, then his hands relaxed and he let the other man go. Nicolai stumbled backward before righting himself. He smoothed down his hair and straightened his suit coat, his face showing disgust at the creases remaining in his shirt. It was the first time Lacey had seen him looking any less than flawlessly composed.

She could almost deem Will's outburst worth it.

Except there was no excuse for either man's behavior. And she was fed up to here with them both.

"Look at you two," she said. "It's just a spitting contest for you, isn't it? Who's got more power, money or influence! Well, believe it or not, I'm all for those things — used for the right purpose, they can do so much good. But at the moment, I want nothing to do with any of them — or you, Nicolai Laslo!"

She whirled around. "And that goes for you, too, Will Proffitt! I'm tired of it, do you hear me? Tired of you all!"

She didn't care that she'd done it again — lost control of her emotions and made a scene right in the middle of town! She didn't care — about Will and his obvious lack of understanding as to what this was about. What *she* was about.

Tears started to her eyes, and Lacey was a scant moment from turning and leaving everyone — the media and townspeople included — to play their little power games when she glimpsed Will's face. It was as impassive and closed as she had ever seen it.

But she knew now who he hid behind that mask, and it was a man who wasn't made of iron, who had been hurt by a woman leaving him without a backward look. Without giving him a chance. If she walked away now, she knew he'd never forgive her.

And she'd never forgive herself. Because she needed something, too, and that was to feel she could be free to be herself with him, free to follow her dream — and stumble and fall if she must — and have him not rush to her rescue or try to run the show, but support her.

If she walked away without trying to get that understanding from Will, she may as well go back to Nicolai, for all that life would be worth living.

She realized of a sudden that every single person and camera was still trained on her, as if everything hinged on her next move.

Well, there was no way she'd give in to public pressure, especially now!

"Didn't you hear me? The show's over, everyone," Lacey said, turning in a circle. "So go home. Please . . . just go back to your homes."

She noticed her parents and Lee echoing her request as they moved through the crowd.

"But which offer will you choose, the count's or the rancher's?" a newsperson asked. "You can't leave us hanging."

"Will you be America's Cinderella — or Abysmal's?" asked another.

At that, a stir of protest started up.

"Silence!" Lacey hollered. A hush descended like the drop of a curtain.

Her gaze swept over the crowd with regal command. So they wanted answers, did they?

"I'll make a statement tomorrow." She pointed at the pavement at her feet. "At noon, right here."

She had no idea what she would say, but she had until tomorrow; she'd think of something.

First, though, she had a matter of greater importance to attend to. Lacey turned to Will. "And you I'd like to see immediately over at the tack and feed."

302

He batted not an eye at her imperious tone but nodded curtly. "Lead the way."

CHAPTER FOURTEEN

Will followed Lacey to the back of the deserted store. If someone was of a mind to loot the whole town, he could carry it off blindfolded. Will would bet cash money that every man, woman, child and animal in Abysmal was out on Main Street right now.

What a scene that'd been! He almost wished for the anonymity of Dallas or Houston or San Antonio, where he could get away for a while from people who knew him and everything about him down to the size of his jeans.

Where he could get away from himself.

It wasn't because Lacey had had to admit in front of the whole town they weren't getting married, even though the scene had been more than a little reminiscent of Lee's forced announcement about him and Lacey over eight years ago. And so what if he had handed Laslo the perfect opening, practically gift wrapped, for such an admission.

304

That wasn't what bothered Will. No, it was the fact that everything he'd worked for and achieved over the past twenty years, everything he was, seemed all for naught, because he knew he couldn't offer Lacey such means as Laslo of furthering this cause so close to her heart. Not here in Abysmal.

She sure hadn't understated the extent of the count's obsessiveness. The man was a certifiable piece of work. And he didn't know the definition of *quit.* He obviously considered Lacey his rightful property, to do with as he wished, and he wasn't going to give up until he had her trapped in his hand like a bird . . . where he'd crush her, once and for all.

The thought of Laslo having the slightest chance of getting to her made Will sick to his stomach.

Oh, he knew she wanted nothing more than to be free of the count — but Laslo had held out to her a mighty tempting morsel in that foundation. Will could see how the prospect excited her. It was everything she wanted and dreamed of. And given that, he knew there was a real danger of her taking Laslo up on his proposal, even if it put her within range of his influence again. Knowing Lacey, with her restored confidence and strengthened sense of purpose — not to mention her passion for her cause — she just might consider it worth having to deal with Laslo again to get the chance to help hundreds of young women around the country.

He had to hand it to the guy. It was a masterful scheme.

So what could *he* come up with to make the difference and get Lacey to stay? Will wondered. From the look on her face, she hadn't been impressed with his own offer.

They reached Lee's office, where Will closed the door behind him, even though there seemed little chance of them being overheard. Lacey marched to the middle of the floor and whirled on him.

"How could you, Will?" she asked. "How could you even begin to think making your offer would help my situation with Nicolai? You had no call to, and you know it! And how could you let him provoke you? You made it look exactly as Nicolai wanted it to, like you're some kind of Daddy Warbucks who thinks he knows better than Orphan Annie what's best for her, or worse, like you're some almighty cattle baron who uses whatever brute force necessary to defend his territory — including his woman!"

"And what rancher wouldn't defend all he held dear when he's got a pack of murderin' outlaws at the door!" Will retorted.

She stalked forward a few steps, indignation radiating from her like heat from a fire. "How many times must I say it? I do not need a man to rescue me, I am not a possession to be wrestled over, and I am *perfectly* capable of making my own decisions about my life, thank you very much! I thought, of everyone, *you* understood that about me and what I need from you!"

"I wasn't trying to possess you or control you *or* rescue you!" Will countered. He flung up a hand. "All right, so maybe I got my dander up and got carried away. Believe me, I'm not too happy with myself for gettin' out of control like that. But I am what I am, Lacey! A take-charge, fix-it kind of man, and while I'm learning how to stand back and let people live their lives, I ask you what was I supposed to do when Laslo started weavin' that web of his? It wasn't just you he was after, it was me and the whole town!"

She pointed to her chest. "But it's me he wants, and he'll use anyone or anything I care about to get to me — Jenna, my parents, my center and yes, you! And if you had let me handle the situation for once, I might've had a chance at saving us all a whole lot of trouble!"

307

"For once?" he echoed incredulously. "Don't tell me I've got the way of things between us wrong, because up to now you've been pretty willing to take full advantage of my offers of help, including helpin' you get over your divorce by lettin' you work out all manner of doubts and worries and fears with me as your testing ground."

He spread his arms as if tendering himself as a stud for hire. "But you know us Proffitts — we don't seem to have the sense of a jackrabbit when it comes to Lacey McCoy!"

Her green eyes darkened to emerald. "Don't you dare insinuate I've ever used you or Lee!"

"Then don't you go and make it sound like I'm the domineering, interfering ring-tailed control freak in this little drama, 'cause we all know Laslo's got that part sewed up tight!"

You could have clothespinned laundry to the stare that hung between them.

Will looked away first, wondering at the desperateness that made his hand shake as he ran it over his face. "Look, Lacey. You've got to see you can't take one step in Laslo's direction."

"I beg your —"

"I know helping girls all over the country

means a lot to you, but it won't do them or you any good if givin' them a chance means havin' anything to do with the man who near to destroyed your life."

Lacey crossed her arms. "Well, at least we agree on one thing."

His shoulders sagged in relief. "So you're not going to take Laslo up on his offer? I mean, it's not like you'd be givin' up on your dream altogether. I meant what I said. You'd have no worries about your center in town makin' it."

She merely looked at him sadly, though he couldn't fathom why. He only had a sense of having failed her somehow.

That desperateness mounted in him again. He felt he had to do something pretty quick, but he didn't know what on earth that could be.

"Lacey —" Will stopped, dropped his chin, hands on his hips, and cleared his throat before trying again. "Lacey, you've got to know I'm not tryin' to control you if I'm sayin' this, but I feel like I'm losing you and I don't know what to do about it. Maybe you can help me, even if I can't help you. Just tell me what you need from me, and I swear I'll do it."

"Will . . . don't you see it's not about that?" she said wearily, as if she were tired

309

of trying to make him understand.

Which caused him to say in complete frustration, "Call me dense, but no, I don't see much of anything at this point!"

Lips compressed, Lacey hugged herself and turned to stare out the window, not responding. She looked so forsaken and forlorn, like she'd just lost her best friend.

He couldn't stand it. Will came up behind her, hesitated, then rested his hands on her shoulders. "Will you at least give me a chance at understanding?" he asked.

Lacey gave a choked cry, turning into his arms and hugging him fiercely, as if for the last time. He held on to her as tightly, cheek pressed to the top of her head. She was so dear to him he could barely comprehend it.

Before he knew it, she let him go and stepped back.

Shoulders back, head held high and looking more like a princess than she ever had, she stood before him.

"It's not that I don't appreciate your help and support, Will," she said. "Because I do. It's meant so much to me over the past months. But what I want . . . *need* more than someone to step in and solve my problems or bear my burdens, is someone with the trust in me and trust in himself to support me through my making my own choices — and mistakes, too — as I go about this lifelong process of becoming me."

An uncanny sense of déjà vu hit him as the finality of her words rang in his head. *I need more than you can give me, Will Proffitt.*

"What're you sayin', Lacey?" he whispered, prepared for the worst.

She glanced down, seeming to concentrate on her hands clasped before her. "What I'm saying is I won't settle for anything less for myself than that sort of complete honesty and trust between me and the man I love."

Will rocked back on his heels. He hadn't been expecting *that.* Had she just said she loved him?

With her eyes downcast and her hands folded before her, she looked the very picture of a martyr at the stake, radiating strength and conviction — while still being completely and utterly vulnerable.

That combination, which to him characterized Lacey McCoy as nothing else could, was something to behold, bringing a lump to his throat the size of Amarillo. Because it was the very essence of a woman in love. Will didn't have to ask to know it as he would his own name.

And, as surely, he knew he loved her, too, in a way he had never believed himself capable — with that total and utter vulner-ability.

The words sprang to his lips to tell her he loved her so, but Will stopped himself at the last second. Not that he wouldn't mean it. Not that he couldn't risk it. It was simply some instinct in him that told him words weren't what Lacey needed from him right now. Which frustrated him, because she'd pretty much forbidden him from doing anything to demonstrate he loved her.

Except this: in one fluid motion, he reached out, snagged her around the waist, and dragged her against him. Their mouths found each other unerringly, and Will held nothing back as he kissed Lacey.

But she deserved better. She deserved complete honesty and truth from him.

So for once it was Will who pulled back first, setting Lacey away from him with a wrenching groan.

She said nothing, her face a one-minute instruction in trepidation. He *hated* that he was even part of the cause of such fear in her! He would have done anything to take it away from her, even if it meant taking it upon himself.

But life didn't work that way, for anyone. Neither did love. Well, if this was what be-ing in love was like, he'd just as soon live without it!

Except, hurt and aching and fearful himself, he'd tried that once, and it hadn't worked.

"So where does this leave us — again?" Lacey asked at last.

"Right where you want to be, is what I'm thinkin'," he said without an ounce of sympathy for either of them. "It's up to you now, Lacey. You wanted choices, you've got 'em. You've just got to figure out behind which door lies the tiger."

Her eyes widened as his words sank in. Pale and wan, Lacey nodded. "As always, I'm thankful for your directness, Will. Now if you'll excuse me, it appears I've got some thinking to do."

He had to cram his fingers into his pockets to keep from reaching for her again as she brushed past him on her way out the door.

It was the single hardest thing he'd ever done in his life, letting her go.

Lacey kept her eyes straight ahead as her father drove the length of Main Street. It was lined with faces, most of them belonging to people she had known all her life. They were faces as familiar to her as her own. She had grown up here. She was one of them. She needed to remember that.

That they would understand.

"You sure you want to go through with this, darlin'?" her father asked, throwing her a worried glance.

"Yes."

Her mother, sitting on her other side, gave her hand a squeeze. "You've said barely a word since last night, Lacey."

"I've been thinking of what I'm going to say."

"You don't have to tell people anything, you know. You've got the public sympathy, hands down. Why, the calls just keep pourin' in from people pledgin' thousands and thousands of dollars to your center, whether it's here in Abysmal or New York City."

"And I'm thankful for that support, Mom, I really am. But I still have to tell them the truth, to make them understand." She clasped her mother's hand tightly to keep hers from shaking. She wasn't afraid so much as nervous. She wanted badly to do the right thing. "I — I don't see how I can do anything else and still live with myself."

She saw her parents exchange worried looks between them, but they said no more, and she blessed them for their silent support. It was exactly what she needed. Exactly.

They reached the spot on Main Street

where, like royalty, she had bid the towns-people all convene in order to hear her words. And like faithful subjects, she saw as she climbed out of the pickup after her mother, they had come as directed. So had the media, even more than yesterday. Nicolai's limousine was parked along the curb, but he was nowhere in sight. Of course, he wouldn't appear until the moment was right. And this moment, for as long as it lasted, was hers.

Yes, Lacey thought, her notoriety as America's Cinderella was good for some-thing.

She was further heartened, as she moved toward the spot where a phalanx of micro-phones had been set up, to hear murmurs of "We're with you, Lacey," and "You jest stand up for yourself, girl," coming from the crowd.

Then Jenna appeared and grasped Lacey's forearm. "Lacey, I had to see you before you got up in front of everyone."

The girl was dressed, Lacey was interested to note, in her old blue jeans and scuffed-up ropers. Of course, so was she.

Jenna caught the direction of her glance and gave an embarrassed laugh. "Those fancy clothes are great for grand entrances, but after I spilled chili down the front of that yellow suit, I decided since I'm stayin' in Abysmal, I'm better off dressing a mite more practical."

"You're staying — for good?" Lacey asked, and Jenna nodded. "But you seemed so excited yesterday by Nicolai's sponsorship of your education."

The girl turned even pinker as, thumbs hooked in her belt loops, she dug her heel into the soft dirt, idly rocking her boot back and forth. "Oh, I don't think it was that as much as bein' dazzled by the thought of comin' back with my head held high."

"It's a great opportunity," Lacey said with a catch in her throat. "One that no one else will be able to give you."

"I know. But I had a good long talk with Daddy last night. He wants what's best for me, and what I could see, after the way Nicolai acted yesterday, was that it wasn't gonna do me any good to take favors from him."

She looked at Lacey with one of those precociously wise looks. "I mean, everyone can use a little support and help. But I kept thinkin' about walking around on that college campus and how I wouldn't feel I belonged there. Not 'cause I was from little ol' Abysmal, Texas," she said hastily, anticipating Lacey's comment. "But because I wouldn't have gotten there on account of my grades or my test scores or any of my other talents."

She turned back into a teenaged girl again as she looked up shyly from beneath her lashes. "So if you'll let me, I'd like to keep helpin' you with your girls' center while I'm busy applyin' for colleges to go to."

Lacey folded her into a tight hug, so proud she could burst. "Believe me, I couldn't do it without you, Jenna." *In so many ways.* Her conviction about what she must do today was strengthened tenfold.

"So I guess the main thing I'm tryin' to say is, do what's right for you, too, Lacey," Jenna said, cheek pressed to hers. "Don't worry about me. I'm going to make it one way or another. Just you watch me!"

"I wouldn't miss it for the world," Lacey whispered.

"Lacey."

She let Jenna go to look up into Lee Proffitt's friendly eyes. "Hello, Lee."

He cocked his head to the side. "Take a walk with me?"

They strolled away from the milling people for a moment of relative privacy.

"Quite a crowd here today, isn't it?" Lee remarked.

"Yes." A quiver of nervousness vibrated

through her, which Lacey countered by observing wryly, "I hope to give them the kind of scene they've come to expect whenever I'm going through a personal crisis."

Lee's smile was sympathetic. "That's sort of what I wanted to talk to you about. Y'see, Will spent half of last night goin' around to people's houses, explaining what this girls' center was about and what it'd mean to the girls in this area, and asking them to show their support for it — and you."

Her jaw dropped. "He did?"

"Yup. And lookie here." He took an envelope out of his back pocket. "It's donations for your center. It's not that people haven't wanted to give before, but now that they know a little bit more of what you're tryin' to do, they think it's a bang-up idea."

He handed her the envelope with a nod. "You'll find just over five thousand dollars in checks in there, with more to come should you need it — you know, if you decide to stay in Abysmal."

Lacey's eyes swam with tears as she held the fat envelope in her hand. Five thousand dollars! It was far from a million, far from the thousands upon thousands pledged from around the country, but more precious to her than all that money put together. "Th-thank you, Lee."

"We aren't a bunch of ignorant bumpkins, y'know. We could see what the count was doing, tryin' to tarnish you and Will and the rest of us. It did the town a powerful lot of good to see Will in a different light yesterday, shed of his usual iron-clad ways. And he pretty much called it like it was with Laslo, earnin' himself a lot of respect for that. Real respect — and not fear."

Dashing away her tears, she glanced around. "Where is Will, anyway? He's coming today, isn't he?"

Lee's gaze was piercing. "I'm not sure, to be honest. I don't know if he knows himself."

She nodded, trying not to get choked up all over again. "I — I understand."

"Do you, Lacey?" he asked abruptly. "Do you understand my brother? He may go overboard sometimes, thinkin' he knows what the people he cares for need better'n they do, but he never stops trying to give them his best, from the bottom of his heart."

Head down, Lacey said nothing. What could she say, especially when a hole was opening up where her own heart used to be?

"Please don't judge me harshly, either, Lee," was all she could say.

"It's never been about judging anyone,

Lacey. You're just you, just as Will's only Will."

She realized he was right. "Yes, that is what it's about it, isn't it? Being accepted — and appreciated — for ourselves."

Lee gave her a chuck under the chin, bringing her head up, and she was relieved when he winked at her, just like in the old days. "You better get goin'. Your public is waiting or champin' at the bit, as the case may be."

Lacey looked around. Indeed, Sheriff Bozeman and a few of his deputized citizens were doing their best to contain a cadre of newspeople behind a bank of sawhorses. When she turned, they set up a caterwaul of clicking shutters and shouts of "Lacey, over here!" and "What's your verdict, Countess?"

She may as well put them out of their misery.

As she walked forward, the door of the black limousine opened and Nicolai Laslo stepped out. He was as tastefully dressed as ever, perfectly groomed, exuding confidence and power and prosperity as if it were his birthright. He stood out like a peacock against the backdrop of the drab brick buildings along Main, against the sea of plain, ordinary-as-sparrows faces.

"Nicolai," she said calmly.

"My dear Lacey."

When he reached for her hand and lifted it to his lips, instead of her usual revulsion rising up in her, she watched him with a curious sort of detachment. The fact was, he no longer had the ability to terrify her. For the first time, she saw Nicolai with eyes unclouded by doubt or fear, sharpened by something much stronger than either. The knowledge gave her courage.

She smiled at him, and the performance began.

"First, Nicolai, I wish to thank you for your generous offer yesterday."

"It is my humblest pleasure to afford you such a means to further your heartfelt cause, if you would but allow me," he answered graciously as ever.

"To think of the kind of good that could be done for girls all over the country with such a foundation . . . well, I'm overcome," Lacey admitted candidly, laying her open hand upon her heart as she immersed herself one more time in the prospect of such an all-encompassing effort. She could practically see each and every girl's face, filled with hope and possibilities.

"You've but to say the word, Lacey, and it's yours," Nicolai said, his tone as sincere as she'd ever heard it, yet he watched her every nuance of expression, Lacey knew, trying to discern her next move. Would she step forward in trust one more time, as she had countless times before? Would she seek vengeance for all the wrongs done her by this man, by relating the emotional injuries she suffered from him? Would she make a show of rejecting his offer outright in a show of defiance? Or would she take it and enter warily into the game of cat and mouse once again?

Lacey had to struggle not to take on that impassive mask as she had thousands of times before to protect herself from such a piercing invasion into her thoughts and emotions. But she had nothing to hide any longer, nothing to fear, no matter what she did.

She had hoped Will would be here to see that — and to hear what she had to say to Nicolai.

Except, Lacey realized of a sudden, it was because of Will that she had to give it one more try. But not this way, not in public.

"Nicolai, could I see you in private?" she asked abruptly.

His "Of course, my dear," was blatantly triumphant.

There was a groan of audible dismay from

the media people. Private meetings did not make good copy. A challenging grumble went up from the townspeople — not at having their curiosity go unrelieved, but at the newspeople's obvious intent to follow Lacey and Nicolai and keep after them for the story.

She didn't care if they did. She was the one who knew what the truth was and that she was doing the right thing.

Then, as she and Nicolai reached the limo, the jabbering dropped suddenly to an awed murmur.

Lacey whipped around, her heart pounding in her throat.

The crowd parted, and a tall, sinewy man walked forward, spurs jingling, Stetson set low on his brow, rugged face impassive.

He looked every inch of his nickname as Iron Will Proffitt.

But Lacey knew — oh, how she knew! — that it was difficult for him to be here, hard for him to have come, because he was a proud man, and this was his town.

She wanted badly to tell him how much his support meant to her, to tell him that she loved him. To tell the whole world that she loved him, and that no matter where she went or what she did, there was no way of removing that love from her heart.

And why shouldn't she come right out with it? What did she have to fear? If Nicolai tried to use her love for Will against her, he would fail. Because love could not be used to control or dominate, it couldn't be leveraged or bargained against. It was stronger than any other force in the universe.

She took a step toward him. "Will —"

He held up a hand. "Wait, Lacey. If you don't mind, I've come to say my piece."

"A-all right."

He shifted his stance so that he stood tall and dignified. "I know I can't make you stay, Lacey," he said, his voice pitched evenly but somehow ringing in the air. "That's for you to decide. And I could probably get you to, by tellin' you I love you with all my heart, except I'd be a skunk to use that kind of admission to sway you."

His gray eyes glowed like pieces of silver. "Only the truth is, I've got nothin' else. I'm as defenseless and exposed as a newborn calf all wet and shiverin' and without a lick of protection from the sun or wind or coyotes. But if I've learned anything from knowing you, it's that when you love someone that much, it's not a weakness but a strength. Because I know you love me, and it hasn't made you one bit less the independent, warm, incredible woman you are. And when you do love someone like that, it'd be next door to criminal to try to hold them down and keep them from spreadin' their wings."

He gave a firm nod. "So you go do what you need to, Lacey. Be what you were born to be. And if that brings you back to me, well then, I'll be here."

Not a twitch, not a blink, not even the stirring of the wind disturbed the silence that had fallen. Lacey herself was paralyzed, although that was more because she was afraid by moving her heart would shatter in a million pieces.

What it had taken him to come here and expose himself so! To make himself so utterly vulnerable for the sake of her.

She'd thought she couldn't love him more. She was wrong.

He was waiting for her answer. Everyone was, including Nicolai.

Numbly, Lacey took a step, then another, and another, until she was running, as if for her life. And then, oh heavenly feeling, she was in Will's arms.

And everyone had their answer — including Nicolai.

Vaguely, Lacey was aware of the din that had gone up, of the townspeople forming an impenetrable circle around them, giving the two of them their privacy, such as it was. From the corner of her eye, she saw the media people converge on Nicolai instead, like a pack of coyotes on an injured rabbit.

But Nicolai was no defenseless animal. With an oath, he shoved a reporter so hard the man lost his balance and would have fallen if his colleagues hadn't caught him. Without a backward glance, Nicolai stalked to his limousine. Once inside, he was inviolate again — for now.

Even safe within Will's embrace, Lacey couldn't help but shiver as the long, black car slunk off.

"You . . . you can still go with him if you want," Will said.

She turned her head to look up at him in amazement. "*Will.* Why would I want to be anywhere but here with you?"

Relief carved a path across his features, and he gathered her back to him as if he'd never let her go. "But I thought . . . that was what you were goin' to talk to Laslo about. Going to New York."

"No! Oh, no!" She pulled away, taking his face between her hands. "I'd come here today to tell my story of what I'd gone through with him — of the emotional abuse and manipulations he used on me to tear

326

me down. I didn't want to expose myself, not just to the whole world not understanding how I could have a fairy-tale life and still not be happy, but to Nicolai, because I knew whatever I said he'd twist it. Then I realized I needed to ask him to let me go, once and for all. To give him — and myself — another chance to try to make him understand, if I could, who I was and what I wanted, to make some kind of an appeal to his intelligence, at the very least, of how he could never have the power over me he wanted, no matter what he did. But I don't think he ever will understand," she said sadly.

Lacey looked up at Will solemnly. "He may come back, Will."

"Then he comes back," he answered without rancor or concern. "There's no defendin' against it, Lacey. You'll deal with the situation when it comes up."

"You're right. I can only live my life the best I can and move forward in trust, striving not to let my fears control me." She stared hard at that lush lower lip of his and tried not to think of how much she wanted him to kiss her right now.

Because she had something else to say. "I can do that now, Will, and you know why?"

"Why?"

"Because I've been blessed with the love of a man who cares enough to look and see what it is I want, what I *need* — and lets me go after it myself. A man who's been at my side within the fortress of my heart, tirelessly helping me put brick upon brick to rebuild myself."

She straightened his collar lovingly. "A can-do kind of man who's helped me design just the right vantage to look out and see what lies beyond the pale and judge its strength. A man whose support gives me the courage to venture out to fight my battles on my own."

Lacey laid her cheek against that wide, solid chest and heard the heart beating inside. "But most of all, a man who keeps the fires burning brightly so I'm able to find my way home to the warmth and understanding waiting for me. *That* is love, as real and deep and true as it gets. And what woman needs Prince Charming when she has such love?"

Lacey closed her eyes, at perfect peace for the first time in her life. Except she had one more thing to say.

"Some day, under the right circumstances and for the right reasons, I'd like to tell the story of what happened to me. I think I'll have to, not so much for myself but for other girls and women, to show them that fairy tales aren't always what they seem to be. That ensuring a happily-ever-after ending takes so much more than gilded palaces and diamond tiaras and a Prince Charming who rides up on a white charger."

"No, sometimes he drives up in a long, black limo," Will pointed out, nestling her against him.

Lacey lifted her head, arching an eyebrow. "Or drives away in one. Which means you win, almighty cattle baron."

Will grinned at the nickname. "And I'd sure be remiss not to've learned something from my Cinderella, and that is how the fairy tale always ends like this."

And with that, Will sealed her mouth with his in a kiss of such power and intensity and unleashed passion Lacey's knees buckled. The whistles and shouts for more went up from the crowd, and Will obliged by catching her up in his arms and twirling her around and around and around as laughter, pure and sweet, bubbled up from inside her.

And with the last breath left in her, Lacey said, "Will Proffitt! You *would* make a scene."

ABOUT THE AUTHOR

Jodi O'Donnell grew up one of fourteen children in small-town Iowa. As a result, she loves to explore in her writing how family relationships influence who and why we love as we do.

A *USA TODAY* bestselling author, Jodi has also been a finalist for Romance Writers of America's RITA® Award and is a past winner of RWA's Golden Heart Award. She lives in Iowa.

The employees of Thorndike Press hope you have enjoyed this Large Print book. All our Thorndike, Wheeler, and Kennebec Large Print titles are designed for easy reading, and all our books are made to last. Other Thorndike Press Large Print books are available at your library, through selected bookstores, or directly from us.

For information about titles, please call:
  (800) 223-1244

or visit our Web site at:
  http://gale.cengage.com/thorndike

To share your comments, please write:
  Publisher
  Thorndike Press
  10 Water St., Suite 310
  Waterville, ME 04901